**Praise for
New York Times and USA Today Bestselling Author

Diane Capri**

"Full of thrills and tension, but smart and human, too."
*Lee Child, #1 New York Times Bestselling Author of Jack Reacher Thrillers*

"[A] welcome surprise….[W]orks from the first page to 'The End'."
*Larry King*

"Swift pacing and ongoing suspense are always present…[L]ikable protagonist who uses her political connections for a good cause…Readers should eagerly anticipate the next [book]."
*Top Pick, Romantic Times*

"…offers tense legal drama with courtroom overtones, twisty plot, and loads of Florida atmosphere. Recommended."
*Library Journal*

"[A] fast-paced legal thriller…energetic prose…an appealing heroine…clever and capable supporting cast…[that will] keep readers waiting for the next [book]."
*Publishers Weekly*

"Expertise shines on every page."
*Margaret Maron, Edgar, Anthony, Agatha and Macavity Award Winning MWA Past President*

# FATAL DEMAND

*by* DIANE CAPRI

Copyright © 2014, 2015 by Diane Capri
All Rights Reserved

Published by: AugustBooks
http://www.AugustBooks.com
ISBN: 978-1-940768-62-5

Original cover design by Cory Clubb
Interior layout by Author E.M.S.

*Fatal Demand: A Jess Kimball Thriller* is a work of fiction, expanded from the Jess Kimball *Flight 12* novella. Names, characters, places, and incidents either are the product of the author's imagination or are used fictitiously, and any resemblance to actual persons, living or dead, business establishments, events, or locales is entirely coincidental.

Published in the United States of America.

Visit the author websites:
http://www.DianeCapri.com
http://www.NigelBlackwell.com

# ALSO BY DIANE CAPRI

## The Hunt for Jack Reacher Series
*(in publication order with Lee Child source books in parentheses)*

Don't Know Jack (The Killing Floor)
Jack in a Box (*novella*)
Jack and Kill (*novella*)
Get Back Jack (Bad Luck & Trouble)
Jack in the Green (*novella*)
Jack and Joe (The Enemy)
Deep Cover Jack (Persuader)
Jack the Reaper (The Hard Way)
Black Jack (Running Blind/The Visitor)
Ten Two Jack (The Midnight Line)

## The Jess Kimball Thrillers Series

Fatal Enemy (*novella*)
Fatal Distraction
Fatal Demand
Fatal Error
Fatal Fall
Fatal Edge
Fatal Game
Fatal Bond
Fatal Past (*novella*)
Fatal Dawn

**The Hunt for Justice Series**
Due Justice
Twisted Justice
Secret Justice
Wasted Justice
Raw Justice
Mistaken Justice (*novella*)
Cold Justice (*novella*)
False Justice (*novella*)
Fair Justice (*novella*)
True Justice (*novella*)

**The Heir Hunter Series**
Blood Trails
Trace Evidence

# CAST OF PRIMARY CHARACTERS

Jessica Kimball

Mandy Donovan

Henry Morris
Roger Grantly
Harriet Grantly
Wilson Grantly

Enzo Ficarra
Luigi Ficarra

# FATAL DEMAND

*When you have eliminated the impossible, then whatever remains, however improbable, must be the truth.*

—*Sherlock Holmes*

---

*I said that. In less words.*

—*Occam*

# CHAPTER ONE

*Montreal, Quebec*
*Sunday, April 20*

*IT'S A GOOD DAY to commit suicide*, the Italian thought as he got off the train at the Bonaventure Metro Station.

Avoiding the Underground City, Enzo Ficarra raised the collar of his supple black leather trench coat with a black-gloved hand and adjusted his fedora before he climbed the stairs up to the sidewalk.

Icy rain pelted his face. Frigid wind matched his mood and further hardened his heart. But it wasn't enough to cool the molten anger seething inside him. He shouldn't be here, in this wretched weather, on Sunday, the first day of spring. He should be in Italy. He should be at Mass.

*Damn Marek.*

Clouds blackened the sky as if he'd entered the city he knew so well at midnight, not mid-morning. He glanced the length of the sidewalk along the *rue de la Cathedrale*. The deserted street was weakly illuminated by streetlights sensitive to darkness. He watched frozen rain melt when it touched the warm street. As the day progressed and temperatures continued to fall, he expected treacherous black ice to capture the city, halting all traffic. He'd be gone by then, and the weather would grant him reprieve from potential pursuit. Not that he expected pursuit. But he was a careful man.

No one walked along the streets. Citizens foolish or determined enough to venture out on such a wicked morning kept to the routes of the Underground City until they reached their churches, reminding him that his own wife and children were at Mass this morning without him. His lips pressed into a grim line. He rarely missed Sunday Mass. His absence would be conspicuous, noted by everyone. This additional grievance further hardened his resolve.

Head down, walking briskly into the blowing sleet, he made his way along deserted sidewalks toward *Les Canard*. The last time he'd been here had been a pleasant Saturday night in July. The streets were busy then, alive until the bars closed at 3:00 a.m. Inside the club, a band played hard rock, dancers crowded the floor, the smell of baking bread wafted out of the kitchen, and the bar bustled with locals chatting in French.

His French was excellent and he had blended into the environment easily, avoiding the English pubs nearby. He always enjoyed the cosmopolitan city. The mix of people and languages, French as well as English, made Montreal better for his work than others. He easily avoided detection here. The city had served him well. God was good.

Now, he rolled his shoulders, lifted his coat collar higher, and waited. He glanced left and right. No pedestrians were near and traffic was sparse.

When the light at boulevard Rene-Levesque changed, he

stepped off the curb and hustled across the street, walking quickly toward Rue Drummond. Marek knew he was coming, but he detected no sign that he was being followed. Marek was not a cautious man. That was one of the many problems between them.

Had he been wrong about Marek, all these years? All through school, the Italian had been stronger than Marek. His Polish friend was short and wiry, but always the weaker as their wrestling matches invariably ended with Enzo the winner. Marek had thus been consigned to follow Enzo's commands and he'd executed each one faithfully.

Which made today's task unpleasant for him.

Resentment fueled Enzo's resolve. Why had Marek made such a disastrous decision? Was it his American wife? A man should never, ever confide in a woman. Women could not be trusted to keep secrets. Nor could men, for that matter. From personal experience, he'd confirmed many times that three people could keep a secret only if two of them were dead.

Whatever the reason, Marek's stupidity had endangered them all. The situation could still be reversed; perhaps Marek had reconsidered.

As he walked, the Italian visualized Marek's club, recalling every detail as sharply as possible. The interior of *Les Canard* was cool, dark and quiet, due to its thick granite walls and dim lighting. When the club was open, the raucous noise inside was muffled.

He arrived at the front entrance. A small sign boasting French calligraphy and an artistically drawn mallard swung from hooks on an iron arm on the left side of the door, squeaking in the gusty wind. The once soft gray granite façade of the club was now dark with decades of soot and city grime. Deep green shades were pulled over the front windows and the closed sign was posted on the door.

All senses alert, he reached for the pitted brass handle and pulled the door open. It had been unlocked for him. He moved soundlessly inside and then flipped the lock to prevent interruption. He stood in the interior foyer of the bar, allowing his vision to adjust.

"Come in, come in!" Marek sat in the shadows facing the door. He rose and hurried toward his guest.

The Italian arranged a friendly smile on his face. They hugged briefly in the Gaelic style.

"Enzo my friend, you are frozen," Marek declared. "Spring, my ass." He shook his head, shrugged at the incomprehensible weather. "Come in, come in. Coffee?"

Marek walked toward the coffee machine behind the bar as he asked the question.

"A double, please." Enzo removed his garments, shook the water off and hung them on the pegs by the door. He grasped his gloves in his right hand.

Marek steamed espresso and poured the rich brew into small white cups, carried the cups with two spoons to the table where small pitchers of cream and sugar waited. He gestured toward the seat he'd vacated, allowing his guest to sit with his back to the wall facing the door. An offer meant to show his partner was welcome, safe here. No one threatened.

They lingered over the fragrant coffee for a few moments, sipping while it was still hot enough to scald their tongues. When the Italian replaced his cup on the saucer, Marek spoke. "Thank you for coming on such a terrible day. We have the place to ourselves."

Enzo nodded, but said nothing.

Marek cleared his throat. He seemed tense, tired. There were dark bags under his eyes. He had not slept well, probably for many nights. Good. Fatigue made him a weaker adversary. "I don't quite know how to begin."

He halted again, drained his espresso, set the cup down on its saucer. He placed both hands on the table in a gesture of trust. He was holding no weapon.

Enzo watched, but kept both hands under the table in his lap. He'd touched nothing except the small white porcelain cup.

Marek flinched when church bells rang in the distance, pealing through the quiet morning, followed by a rumble of thunder. He grinned a bit, embarrassed.

The Italian prodded. "What did you want to see me about, Marek?"

Marek's hand shook when he lifted his cup to his lips. He seemed chagrined to realize it was empty, and set it back down. He took a deep breath and said softly, "You and I, we have only a few open projects just now. All are at the stage to be easily completed. The money we've received has been deposited to your Swiss accounts."

After a pause, Marek continued, "I must quit, you see."

"Oh?" Enzo conveyed mild surprise he did not feel.

"You know my second son was born last month." Marek gestured with his head toward the ceiling because his family lived upstairs, above the club. "He has a brother, like you now. He needs a respectable father with a business he can inherit. Like you have in Tuscany. A legitimate enterprise," he whispered as a man with dry mouth does.

In the quiet, following the muffled sound of thunder, Enzo understood. The wife had made Marek do this. Women stupidly protected their children, failing to appreciate the consequences, and men followed their wives even into disaster.

"I see."

Marek loosened the top button of his gray flannel shirt and rubbed his neck with his left hand. "I know what we agreed. With this kind of work, a lifelong commitment is required. And you know I will always be loyal to you. Completely. But…" He swallowed. "But I must stop. We've had many successful projects together. I've bought this club. It's paid for. All mine now. And I have a home. Here. To raise my sons. Be a husband. Build my own family. You understand, Enzo my friend," he paused a beat. "Yes?"

The Italian drained the last drops from his cup. He smiled sorrowfully at his oldest friend. "Of course. I want you to be happy. Family is important. I love children. You know that. You must have a large family, and a wonderful life. Like I do. Naturally." He laughed, as if anything else would be too absurd to contemplate.

Marek laughed along, shakily. He pulled out his wallet and displayed pictures of his new son, his three-year-old boy, and beautiful wife.

"They know nothing of my work for you," Marek volunteered.

Which meant that he'd told his wife everything.

Enzo's anger grew hotter. Marek had jeopardized not only his own family, but the entire business.

He took a deep breath, and they talked of earlier times. They shared stories. Enzo asked about Marek's plans for the future. Eventually the Italian glanced at his watch. "I must go. My train departs soon. My own family waits. But I will miss you, old friend."

His words flowed easily, though he never allowed himself such sentiments. Not even with his own brother.

The two men stood. Enzo reached a hand into his pocket and pulled out the capsule, hiding it in his left palm. They moved closer to hug again, Marek foolishly relaxed.

The Italian quickly turned and grabbed Marek by the forehead from behind, cruelly twisting his neck and pulling him against his shoulder.

Marek gasped, and in that instant, Enzo forced the capsule into his open mouth and pressed Marek's jaw closed using the butt of his other hand.

Brief comprehension registered in Marek's eyes as the capsule broke and cyanide drained into his mouth. He wrestled and fought, but like in their younger years, he lost. He tried to breathe through his nose. His arms flailed, beating on Enzo's chest.

"I'm sorry, old friend, that you have chosen to betray me," Enzo said, holding Marek's chin shut lest any of the poison seep out.

Marek blinked his eyelids one last time. The poison had done its job as it always did. He slumped to the floor, eyes open, staring at his friend until gravity dragged his eyelids down.

Enzo knelt, felt Marek's carotid artery for a pulse and found none. He waited ten minutes to be sure Marek was dead and that no one had heard the encounter.

He had one more task. Enzo stood, glanced around briefly. Where would Marek hide his electronic equipment? He searched behind the bar with no luck.

A loud thump followed by a crying baby sounded from the apartment above.

How could that be? Marek's family was upstairs?

"Idiot!" he swore. Marek had been told that there should be no one else present. He couldn't follow directions anymore. Another good reason to have eliminated him.

Enzo hurried now, completed his search of the entire club, finding nothing. He could not leave without Marek's computer and cell phones. There must be no trace of his connection to the Italian's business. He had no choice. He must search upstairs.

Damn Marek.

Quickly, he pulled on his gloves, walked back to his coat and pulled a .22-caliber Smith & Wesson and suppressor from deep pockets. He reached for the extra magazine, dropping it into his trouser pocket. He assembled the suppressor as he hurried from behind the bar, into the kitchen, and then climbed the stairs to Marek's apartment.

Halfway up he heard a woman's voice, "Marek? Is that you?"

Enzo hustled up the remaining stairs and entered the living room, startled to find Marek's wife seated directly across from the archway, looking straight at him, nursing the new baby.

Enzo had not seen the woman in the flesh before. Marek had thought her plain features, and horsey face, beautiful. Another mistake.

Her eyes widened, not in surprise, but recognition. She knew what Enzo looked like.

He scanned the room. The apartment was empty but for the wife, the infant, and Marek's toddler seated beside her on the couch, sleeping with its thumb in its mouth.

Now, all options were canceled. She'd seen him, and would know that her husband had not committed suicide. She would identify him to the authorities. Not an insurmountable problem, but an unnecessary one. Easier to stop her now.

The moment Marek had revealed them both, her husband had signed her death warrant. What followed now was blissfully not the Italian's choice, but white-hot anger fueled him nonetheless.

"Damn Marek!" Enzo spoke aloud.

He raised his pistol. She gasped. He shot twice. The forehead. Small holes. Her head bounced backward against the sofa. A bit of blood pushed out from the two bullet wounds. Her heart still pumped, she wasn't quite dead. He waited for the message of her demise to reach her heart.

Despite the gun's noise, the toddler still slept. If he didn't awaken, he would live. The infant, too. He lay in the cradle of her arms, resting on a sturdy pillow, nursing, unaware of the mother's death. He had seen his own infants feed and he knew how intent they could be on the nipple. He was curious as to how long the mother's milk might flow, but he had no time to watch. He still had to search the apartment.

Enzo glanced at his watch. Four minutes had elapsed since he'd climbed the stairs. His own breathing was normal. Very little exertion in the project so far. He strode through the four-room apartment, checked the closets quickly. There was no one else. No more witnesses to eliminate.

He considered where Marek might have kept his electronics. Since Marek's wife knew about his work, he probably had a small desk in the apartment somewhere. He went quickly from room to room until he located Marek's desk in the back hallway. The laptop was turned on, connected to the Internet. Marek's cell phones were also on the desk.

He pulled the cables from the laptop, folded it closed, tucked it under his left arm, and slipped the phones into his trouser pockets. It took only a few moments. He considered whether

Marek might have hidden anything that would incriminate either of them here. If so, he knew he couldn't find it quickly.

He'd have to take that chance and the lack of choice Marek left him further confirmed his actions. No, he didn't regret the kills. He regretted only that Marek had been such a fool in the end.

Enzo turned and hurried back down the stairs. Despite his gloves, he wiped the gun using the tail of his silk shirt, knelt and placed the gun in Marek's hand, making sure to imprint it properly. Then he shot a round into the baseboard of the wooden bar by pulling Marek's finger on the trigger to assure there would be gunshot residue on his hand. He dug the bullet from the wood and dropped it into his pocket.

The Italian surveyed the scene, recalling his movements, making sure he'd left no evidence that might cause suspicion or lead back to him.

The scene was perfect.

He picked up the coffee cup and saucer he'd used and, to be cautious, the extra spoon.

He was satisfied he'd touched nothing else. No fingerprints nor DNA was left behind. The scene accurately depicted an insane, sleep-deprived father who killed his family and then himself on a cold and depressing Sunday morning.

The Italian donned his long coat, turned up the collar and set the fedora on his head. He flipped the small button on the door handle that would lock it again when he closed the door behind him.

He retraced his route through sleet-slicked streets, the cup and saucer still warm in his pocket.

# CHAPTER TWO

*Dallas, Texas*
*May 10*

JESS KIMBALL WAITED IN the private visitor room at the jail normally reserved for meetings between inmates and their lawyers. She wanted to write this scene effectively for her *Taboo Magazine* readers, but she found nothing compelling about the room. No windows, no noises. No atmosphere of any kind. Thick walls kept the world outside and the criminals inside. Exactly what a jail should be, even if it was too good for the lowlife she was going to meet.

She heard a spritzing noise and noticed the cloying citrus aroma. A quick glance around the ceiling revealed the automatic air freshener in the corner behind her chair.

The door opened. A deputy came in, and looked around. "All clear. Send him in."

The inmate, Stosh Blazek, entered unrestrained. He was forty-three years old. Average in every way. Average height, average weight, average hair and eyes. Not one thing remarkable about him. It was his very averageness that caused senior citizens to trust him, and follow him deeper and deeper into heartbreaking financial losses from which they never recovered.

Jess hated thieves, but those who stole from the elderly were as bad as they came. At that moment, staring at Blazek, she knew she'd met the poster-boy for heartless scum.

On a tip, her publisher had sent her to the first heartbreaking interview six weeks ago—Sam Nelson, a proud ninety-four-year-old World War II veteran, and his wife Jane. Sweet people. Hard working. They'd outlived their friends and two of their children, but they were survivors. They hadn't let hardship or grief derail them. Until they met Blazek.

Blazek had targeted them, tugged on their heartstrings until Jane persuaded Sam to contribute to Blazek's phony African AIDS victims' charity. Starving children needed their meager savings, Blazek said. Sam's generous nature overcame his good sense.

Blazek had cheated Sam and Jane out of every cent they owned. When Jess met them, they were eating canned fish because they were too proud to collect food stamps. Their home had been pledged to Blazek and they were being evicted. Jane spent the entire interview crying and Sam patted her shoulder because that was the only thing he could really do.

Jess promised to help them. She had uncovered and interviewed a grand total of forty-six of his victims. After their lifetimes of hard work, Blazek had hounded them all to ruin. He took everything from them. Their money, their dignity.

From some, he stole their will to live. For others, Jess had been too late. She'd heard time and again how desperation caused Blazek's victims to murder their spouses and commit suicide.

Sam Nelson had done that two days after Jess interviewed him. Before Jess could get Sam and Jane the help she'd promised.

She hated Blazek and every lying piece of crap like him.

Too bad he didn't get the death penalty this morning. He deserved it. And if Jess had anything to say about it, she vowed he'd never walk out of here a free man again.

"You know the drill, Blazek. You're being watched and recorded by that camera in the corner over there. You have fifteen minutes," the deputy said, before he turned and left.

Jess glanced at the camera again. The red light on the bottom meant it was operating.

She sat with her back to it, making sure Blazek was facing the lens. If he said anything that could be used against him, she wanted an airtight recording.

She kept her hopes in check. Unlikely he'd say anything important, but she'd had luck with smarter criminals than Blazek before. She couldn't fail Sam and Jane or the others. She simply could not, would not fail.

"Thank you for coming, Ms. Kimball," Blazek said. Even his voice was deceptively average.

Her stomach soured. She felt bile rising in her throat. "Why did you want to see me again, Mr. Blazek?"

"Call me, Stosh. Everybody does," he replied, automatically, as he had when she'd met him before, as if he'd said it thousands of times. He probably had. Probably in this very room.

Back when he routinely perched on the lawyer side of the table instead of the criminal side where he sat now.

She might have engaged in a contest of wills with him under different circumstances. But time was short. "Why did you want to talk to me, Mr. Blazek?"

"I saw you in the court room. You know I've read your work since we talked the last time. You really do care about crime victims. Like me." His expression revealed no irony at all.

She clenched her jaw tight to keep her mouth from falling open. How could he possibly believe he was any sort of victim? The guy had brass balls, for sure. "You pled guilty. Fraud, larceny, and grand theft. And a few other offenses. They couldn't make murder charges stick. You lucked out with that plea bargain. How does that make you any kind of victim?"

"You don't understand."

"I understand you cheated a long string of elderly people, Mr. Blazek. The ones who weren't so devastated that they committed suicide will live out their lives in hopeless poverty." She kept her voice level and stone cold. "You're the polar opposite of the kind of person I want to help."

He pounded his fist on the table. "I had no choice! Don't you understand that? You need to stop them before another life is ruined forever!"

Jess stared at the man. Could he be such a stranger to reality? Or maybe he felt betrayed. Some thieves did after they were caught.

The air freshener spritzed again and the sickly sweet citrus aroma filled the room.

She lowered her chin and narrowed her eyes. "Stop who?"

"They tricked me. They took everything I had. They said I'd get the money back that I borrowed from my clients to help them. But they lied." The pouty child he'd probably been a few decades ago seeped through in his aggrieved complaints. "And now they're going to kill my friends."

"Who is 'they'?" She glared at him. "And who do you think they're going to kill?"

He shrank back and shrugged. "Who knows? Could be any of them."

"Any of who?"

"They took everything from me, and—"

"No one took anything from you, Mr. Blazek. You willingly gave away what you had, and then cheated and stole from everyone who trusted you so you could chase a pot of gold at the end of a fraud." Unmoved, Jess stated the hard truth. "You crippled seniors who will never recover from it. You *pled* guilty because you *are* guilty."

"They were going to kill me," he whined.

She leaned back and crossed her arms over her chest. "Stop sniveling and prove it."

"It's an international crime ring. Italians. Maybe even Mafia—"

"Mafia?" Jess curled up one side of her lips as if he'd said *Martians*. "That's the best you've got?"

"They target businessmen like me. Rip us off so they can get access to our accounts. They promise a return on our investment that never materializes until we're tapped out. And then...then...well, they don't stop. They wring everything out of you. Everything. And then they go after anyone who knows you."

"Italians? The Mafia?" She shook her head. "I heard your testimony, and I believe it's the first honest thing you've said." She leaned forward. "You were the center of the crime ring. You're the one who cheated and stole from those people."

"They made me do it!" He shouted, standing up abruptly, knocking the metal chair over behind him. It clanged against the floor.

She shrugged, still relaxed in her seat. "Uh huh. Why didn't you cooperate with the FBI then?"

"I did! I did, I tell you!" Still shouting.

Calmly, Jess replied, "And?"

"And they failed. The FBI failed to find them, and failed to stop them." He glared at her, eyes wild, nostrils flared.

Jess looked up into his face. She pointed to his chair. "Sit down, you're making my neck sore."

Blazek continued to glare. The citrus air freshener squirted. The big clock on the wall ticked off a few seconds.

She waited silently until he finally bent over, picked up the chair, and reseated himself.

Only then did Jess ask, "Stop who, precisely? Because that's the problem with your story, isn't it? There's no one involved in these thefts except you and your victims."

He crossed his hands on top of the table and leaned in. "Talk to Morris. He's got the information I gave him. He'll tell you what happened. And you'll see I'm telling the truth."

He meant FBI Special Agent Henry Morris. Jess had already interviewed him twice on the phone. He wasn't at all sympathetic to Blazek. "Tell me the names of the friends you're worried about."

He slid a scrap of paper across the table. A list of five names in tiny, precise, cursive script.

She glanced at the names. She'd come across none of them during her investigation. Which meant he was probably lying again.

"You didn't name your friends or accuse the FBI of failing in court when you pled guilty this morning."

Blazek slumped and shook his head. "People said I was greedy, wanted to get rich quick. That's not true. I got in way over my head. But I was gullible. And desperate."

"You're still alive so you're not half as desperate as the old folks you cheated." Jess figured Blazek was about the least gullible person she'd ever met. But she'd buy the desperate part. He had wriggled and squirmed in every way possible before his trial like a trout on a hook. But he didn't get away.

"Do you have any idea what it's like being the son of a wealthy man?"

Jess snorted a laugh. She hadn't seen that one coming.

Blazek pushed his chin out. "Well, it's not as great as you might think. Especially if you're a constant screw up, like I was. My dad gave me a viable business before he died. I ran it into the ground."

"Common story." She pressed her eyelids closed a moment. She was tired and she needed a break and she had a long way to go tonight. There was still a lot to do. Every minute she spent here was a minute she wouldn't spend searching for her son. Blazek wasn't worth another second of sacrifice.

She picked up her notepad and pen, and tossed them into her oversized messenger bag. Time to go.

"But then I got a chance that would have saved me. Saved my business. And I took a risk." Blazek raised his intensity. "You would have, too. Anybody would have." He lowered his gaze to the table, maybe trying to appear contrite.

Jess wondered if he'd taken acting lessons or if he was simply another manipulative sociopath with a lot of experience at conning others.

Either way, she figured he rarely felt contrite at all. He felt nothing remotely like empathy for his victims. This wasn't Blazek's first trip to the justice system rodeo. Only this time, he was getting gored.

Jess shrugged as if to say *Who cares?* The wall clock said she'd only been talking to Blazek for five minutes. It seemed a lot longer. He was a waste of her time.

During the next part of Blazek's performance, he lowered his voice as if he was embarrassed or ashamed, like a normal person would be. Or maybe he wanted her to think he was telling her something secret.

"The thing is, they got access to my books. I had client names in there and some were prominent business people. A few were friends for years, since school. I didn't even know they'd been contacted." He raised his head and looked directly into her eyes. Was this supposed to be sincerity, now? "My friends got into the deal because they believed if I was in, the deal was legitimate."

The citrus spray squirted again and the heavy scent was nauseating. Or maybe sitting in the same room with Blazek was the cause of her stomach's revolt.

Jess stood up. "But the deal wasn't legitimate. You knew that. And you didn't warn them? Some friend."

"By the time I found out, they were already involved. There was nothing I could do." He stopped pleading briefly. His eyes were glassy with tears.

Jess had met sociopaths before who could cry at will. Perhaps tears were an effective weapon on some people. But not her. She'd cried too many of her own.

"So you're saying that we haven't found all of your victims yet. In addition to the senior citizens you stole from, you also created a cadre of thieves just like you who could steal from their victims, too." She sneered. "What a guy."

"Just before I was arrested, I lost contact with my friends." He blinked his tears away. "I'm worried about them, Ms. Kimball. Very worried."

Maybe he was. Or maybe he had a different agenda. Either

way, it was none of Jess's concern. She was done here.

The buzzer sounded and the door opened. The deputy held the door with his hip. "Come on, Blazek. Time to go."

Blazek looked directly into Jess's eyes again. "Be careful, Ms. Kimball. These Italians are bastards. Ruthless." His tone was as hard as blood diamonds. "Don't think they won't kill. They will. Unless you do something about it."

"Thanks for the tip. Good to know." Jess turned off the recorder and dropped the phone into her bag.

Blazek walked ahead of the deputy as they left the interview room. Jess stared at the door after it closed, wondering whether she should believe anything he'd said.

Now what?

Wrap it up and move on.

Liars like Blazek always had another excuse ready when the last one flopped. Only gullible people believed them. Jess was a lot of things, but gullible she was not.

She glanced at the clock on the wall under the security camera. She was booked on a flight back to Denver in four hours. Plenty of time to nail down Blazek's latest excuse and close her story with a bit of extra flair. She had time to burn.

Maybe she should have her head examined, but she couldn't think of a single legitimate reason not to follow up on Blazek's last statement.

Cases like this one, where nothing she did could make a significant difference to his victims, sucked her soul. She needed a break from the never-ending supply of heartless scum like Stosh Blazek who never, ever picked on somebody their own size.

After today, she promised herself, she'd take a break. Before her work snapped her in half and she was no good to anyone.

Tonight, she'd wash off Blazek's slime with a good, long shower. Tomorrow she would file her article, then take a few days off. She'd already requested the vacation time and she'd planned to spend it looking for Peter, as she always did.

But maybe she'd take a real break this time. First time in years. To clear her mind and renew her senses.

Maybe a quiet hotel in a remote town. Near a river or a lake. The water soothed and relaxed her the way nothing else did. She could do that, couldn't she?

But not a place so remote as to be cut off from the world. One of her investigators could call. She wouldn't ever be totally unavailable. Not until she found Peter, until she knew he was safe.

She sighed. Maybe she'd come back to her search for Peter with fresh ideas, and to *Taboo* less weary, not as jaded. She'd heard vacation time could refresh and renew like that, but she'd never tried.

For now, she'd finish the job she came to do. She'd close up Blazek's coffin tighter than a sealed air cryovac capsule. She couldn't undo the harm Blazek had caused, but she might be able to prevent more harm from flowing through his crimes.

She looked at the names he'd given her: Kowalski, Warga, Zmich, Supko, and Grantly. They weren't unique names, but there couldn't be that many Wargas, Zmichs, or Supkos in the country. She included their first names and texted the list to her assistant with a request for a search.

A few minutes later, she got a list back. Wargas, Zmichs, and Kowalskis popped up all over the country, but there was only one Joshua L. Supko on the list and he lived in Texas in a town with the unlikely name of Highland Village.

She Googled the address, and his house appeared on the map not half an hour from her present location.

She sat in her rental car considering her options. If she were to approach Supko, she'd need a good reason to get him to talk.

The Blazek story had been on the news, and point blank asking the man if he'd been involved in a scam was a sure way to get thrown out.

She kicked herself for not finding out how Blazek and Supko knew each other. Her dislike of Blazek had clouded her judgment. It was a loose end, and she should have picked at it, found out everything she could before moving on.

She sighed. With nothing else to go on, she'd have to play the dumb girl reporter, and hope the man liked to talk.

It wouldn't be the first time a man had boasted how much he knew and how much she didn't. The best strategy she'd found was to let them underestimate her as long as she could stomach the ruse.

# CHAPTER THREE

JESS FOLLOWED HER GPS'S directions to Highland Village. As she suspected, there was no sign of any highlands, the place was flat for miles around. Despite the lack of geographic features, it had some character, and there were more lakes and ponds than seemed likely for a state that frequently boasted triple-digit heat waves.

In an area that could certainly be called upscale, Joshua Supko lived in a gated neighborhood another step up the scale.

Following a Lexus through the gates, she smiled and waved like a ditzy blonde at a security guard as he tried to stare through her windows. She kept to the posted twenty mile-per-hour speed limit in the hope the man would be fooled into believing she belonged inside the walls.

The houses varied dramatically in scale. French chateaus nestled beside monumental Pueblos and English cottages with what appeared to be genuine thatched roofs. Lawn crews worked in gangs. Now and again she passed a bright green VW Beetle with the name of some house cleaning company emblazoned on the side.

She eased the rental over a narrow humpback bridge, and the GPS announced her destination was on the right.

Supko's house stole its style from the bold straight lines and simplicity of Frank Lloyd Wright. Low rise windows stretched across seemingly unlikely portions of the building, and a mixture of wood and concrete highlighted a stark, but sympathetic, contrast of man and nature.

She angled her budget rental car into a wide horseshoe driveway and parked behind a pair of Mercedes SUVs with vanity plates. She wasn't planning to fool anyone into believing she lived in the neighborhood.

Jess grabbed her bag and walked to the double front doors. A panel on the side contained a speaker and a camera. She straightened her back, smiled, and pressed the button.

Gongs chimed deep inside the building. She waited. Ten seconds. Twenty. Thirty, forty. She reached for the button. The speaker crackled into life.

"Yes?" said a male voice.

"Joshua Supko?"

"Who is this?"

She kept up her smile. "A friend."

"Really. What name did you use at security?"

She feigned surprise. "Security?"

"Yeah. The people with guns at the front gate. The ones I'm calling right now."

"Wait."

The speaker clicked off.

She stabbed the button. "Wait, wait. I'm a friend. I…I'm Jessica Kimball, from *Taboo Magazine*. I—"

The speaker clicked back on. "A friend? Or a reporter looking for gossip?"

"I…I have a message. I talked to a friend of yours. He's worried about you."

"Really?"

"Yes, and…can we talk?"

"No. I've called security. You can talk to them."

Jess looked behind her. A Ford Escape bounced over the humpback bridge.

She looked back at the speaker. "Joshua, Stosh Blazek thinks you might be in some danger."

The voice in the speaker blew out a long breath. "Jessica whatever your name was, you're not that much of a friend."

She held up her hands. "Okay. I'm not really a friend, I'm just—"

"Let me set you straight. We bought this house from the bank. A repossession. A good deal. Nothing more. Got it?"

"Er…okay."

"We never met this Supko guy who owned the place before. I don't know him, or anything about him. I've only seen his name on some of the papers."

The Ford Escape screeched to a halt in the driveway.

"So, you don't know anything about where to find him?"

The speaker clicked off.

Two guards got out of the Ford. One held a pump-action shotgun in front of his ample belly. Texas, she thought, as she dialed up the innocence in her smile.

"Hands where we can see 'em," said the gray-haired man with the shotgun.

She held her palms out at shoulder height. The second man was younger. Bigger. Bulked up. He'd have been a good candidate for a beefcake calendar if they used his picture only from the neck down. His cheekbones had been broken sometime in his past, leaving his face with a broad, flat profile.

He came close enough. The nameplate on his shirt said James Polar. He patted her down, roughly but with an exaggerated attempt to prevent a sexual assault claim.

She nodded to the bag. "There's a gun inside. I have a permit. Concealed carry."

"ID?" said Polar.

She nodded to the bag again. "Zip pocket. Driver's license, and my press card is in there. Jessica Kimball, *Taboo Magazine*."

Polar grunted. "Damn press." He held out his palm. "Keys."

She fished around in her pocket and pulled out the huge plastic key tag. She dropped the keys into his hand.

He opened the rear of the Ford. She stepped in and he closed the door.

A Plexiglas barrier separated her from the front of the vehicle. The older man with the shotgun drove the Ford back to the main gate.

Polar drove her rental and parked it in a yellow-hatched spot just beyond the gates.

They hustled her into the guard station, the shotgun in plain view at all times.

A counter divided the room in two. Behind the counter were a bank of video monitors, radios, and blinking lights. In front of the counter was nothing other than a row of hard plastic chairs against the far wall. She sat in a corner.

Polar left to stand guard at the main gate. The older man went through her bag, emptying the contents into a plastic tray. He looked at her press card, and made several phone calls. Thirty minutes later, he stuffed her belongings into her bag, and handed it to her. "Don't come back."

Normally, she would have argued about the search, but she still needed information. She took the bag, looked at the silver nameplate above his shirt pocket, and gave him a tentative smile. "I didn't mean to cause trouble, Mr. Barnes."

He sneered. "Bull. You knew exactly what you were doing. Something we'll have to explain to our boss tomorrow morning."

"I'm—"

"Every time one of the residents calls about an intruder, we've screwed up. We're the ones who get dumped on." He rubbed the back of his neck.

"Mr. Barnes," she frowned, "I just wanted to talk to Joshua Supko. A friend of his thinks he might be in serious danger."

"You've heard of the police, right?"

"I have a contact at the FBI. I'm going to talk to him, too." She sighed. "I just thought it might be important to tell Mr. Supko first."

Barnes stowed the shotgun underneath the counter. "I don't think anything's very important to Mr. Supko these days, is it?"

"Er…" Her eyes narrowed and she bit her lip.

He did a double take. "Are you kidding?"

She shook her head slowly.

"Some reporter you are." He rolled his eyes. "Supko's dead."

# CHAPTER FOUR

JESS GLANCED AT BARNES before she cleared her throat and swallowed. "When?"

"Two months and six days ago, why?"

She cocked her head. Her gaze narrowed. "That's an amazingly accurate count."

"Not likely I'll forget." He rubbed the back of his neck again. "That was the last time I got grilled. Almost lost my job over it."

Jess blinked rapidly trying to clear her head. What the hell was he talking about?

"My boss takes this job seriously. He thinks we're really law enforcement around here." Barnes spoke slowly, as if he doubted her mental capacity. "The same boss who is going to turn up and chew me out again tomorrow."

She nodded. "I really am—"

"Yeah, yeah. Anyway, I'm hardly likely to forget Supko, am I?" He paused and dropped the hostility down a notch. "I'm the one who found him."

"What happened? To Supko, I mean?"

"You think this place is an open book or something?" Barnes looked at her steadily. He jerked his thumb over his shoulder pointing to the driveway. "Check out that fence with the gates, sweetheart. We're paid to keep private lives private around here."

She nodded again. "Course. I didn't know he'd died. One of his friends was worried about him, and I, er, offered to check in on him."

Barnes frowned. "What friend?"

Jess shook her head.

"Can't say, huh?" Barnes paused to give her a chance to speak, maybe. She didn't. "It was in the papers. Him dying, I mean."

"Locals?"

"Local what? Cops?"

She blinked. "Papers."

"Yeah, guess it wasn't big news around the globe or anything. Guy wasn't a celebrity." He gave a single nod. "But they didn't get any of it from me. Not directly. You know. People talk, and—"

"And what?"

"Once a story gets out," he shrugged, "people don't care if they got it from the source or not."

"You mean, you?"

"Yeah. Well, I told you. I discovered him."

"How did that happen?"

Barnes glanced out of the window on the top of the door. His colleague, Polar, pushed a button to open the gate and waved a black BMW through.

"Those other people," Barnes gnawed his lower lip and lowered his voice. "They got paid."

Jess cocked her head. *I see what you want.*

Whatever Barnes had to say, he probably told the police. In a very short time, she could find the local office and request the information herself. If the case was closed, local cops would probably give her whatever she asked for. No reason to withhold anything, assuming Supko's death was a straight suicide.

Jess took a deep breath and glanced at the clock. Paying Barnes would be quicker. Easier to hear the story now than deal with an unknown police department, and whatever red tape they might dream up. She could put this to bed now and file her story on time. Or chase what would be a secondary source anyway, just like Barnes said.

She pulled a hundred dollars from her wallet, and slid it across the counter. "Tell me."

Barnes looked at the money and squirmed. He didn't reach for the crisp Franklin.

Jess frowned. "You don't want it?"

"That Glock." He gave a nod toward the weapon. "Nice piece. Always wanted one of those."

"It's got sentimental value." She reached for the bill. "It's also a very expensive piece."

Barnes opened his mouth and nodded again toward the gun before he closed his lips without uttering another word.

She pulled two fifty-dollar bills from her wallet and added them to the Franklin. "Two hundred, and not the Glock. Owning that particular gun is very important to me." She held the money out at arm's length.

Barnes checked out the window to be sure his colleague wasn't watching. His hand snaked out and grabbed the bills. "And no names, right?"

She nodded. "So, tell me."

Barnes folded the money and shoved it into his front pocket as if he thought she might try to snatch it back.

"It was late afternoon. Just after five. We got a call." He jerked his thumb toward a monitor with a layout of the properties on the estate. "The Supko house. Lit up. Flashing red." He leaned forward. "That means it's an emergency. So, we do what we're supposed to do. Police, fire, ambulance. They're all on speed dial. We call as we race over to the house. Got there in one minute. Ninety seconds, tops."

She nodded.

"Well, Mrs. Supko is going nuts. She's got this bunch of kids all making noises in her front room. And she's practically locking them in there. Got the door closed. Yelling at them not to come out. We had to calm her down. She's freaking out." He stopped for a long breath. "So she takes us out back. You saw they have a big place. Sprawling. Giant patio bigger than my apartment. And a huge pool. And Mr. Supko. He's just there. In the pool."

She made a mental note to obtain photos or video of the outside of the Supko property. "Drowned?"

Barnes shook his head. "Not actually in the pool. He's on one of those," he waved both hands in front of his stomach to help him find the word and failed to pull it up, "floating recliner things. Floating on the water. Like he's sunbathing. Got a drink in a kind of stand on the," he waved his hands again, stretching the air between them, "floating thing."

"Was he already…"

"His head's leaning over," Barnes nodded vigorously, "and he's got one arm in the water."

"He could have been asleep."

"No. No chance." Barnes shook his head. "He was gone."

"You checked?"

"Yeah. Well, that's when the fire department showed up. Came straight through the house. Jumped in the pool. Gear on and everything. Straight in the water. Pulled the floaty thing to the side." He took another breath. "I helped lift him out. And...yeah, he was gone for sure. Then the police and ambulance arrived and it turned into a madhouse for sure."

Jess wondered exactly what she'd bought for her two hundred dollars that a quick Internet search would have failed to turn up. "Any conclusions reached at the scene?"

"Not then." Barnes shrugged. "They took a load of prints and pictures and all that at the time. But eventually, suicide, they said. Cyanide. Reckon he took a dose with his drink, and went to sleep on the floaty thing."

She reviewed his tale in her mind for a couple of seconds. "Is that what you think?"

Barnes shrugged again. "I mean, they're the experts, right?"

She inched closer to the counter. "You gave your report to the police?"

"Yeah."

She raised her eyebrows. "Was there anything you didn't tell them?"

"Nope." Barnes shook his head. "Told them everything. Just like I told you."

"*Exactly* like you told me?" She cocked her head and narrowed her gaze until he squirmed. "Nothing else?"

"Yeah, and...well, later, you know, I found out some other stuff." He stuffed his hands in his pockets.

"Like what?"

"Mrs. Supko, she'd taken her kids down the street that morning. The neighbors were having a kid's birthday party."

"What about Mr. Supko?"

"He was helping to set up all morning and then they had the party all afternoon." He lowered his voice. "But before that, Mr. Supko, he goes out in the morning. Nine o'clock. Like usual. Only he comes back. Ten thirty-seven."

"And that was unusual?"

"Oh, yeah. He's a late night bird. Works all hours. But he came back. It's in the book. On video, too." He stopped and glanced around.

"And?"

He dropped his voice lower. "Only there was someone in the back of his car. Can't see it too well on the film, but I could," he gestured to the gate where his colleague stood now, "from out there."

"Did you tell the police about the man in the back seat?"

He nodded firmly this time. "And they looked at the tapes."

"Who was the man?"

Barnes shook his head. "Don't know. Never seen him before. And the police? They said they couldn't be sure. The tape was kind of hard to see. But I know what I saw."

Jess waited a second but he said nothing else. "So, Supko comes back early, with a stranger, and is found dead a few hours later."

Barnes nodded again.

"And the police didn't think that was suspicious?"

"No one else saw the guy."

"What did he look like?"

"A guy. It was just a glimpse. You know," he glanced at her purse, "cars can go by pretty quick."

She nodded toward his pocket. "I've already made my contribution."

He frowned. "Er…yeah, right."

"Was there anything else suspicious?"

Barnes frowned and pretended to think. "When we got there, he'd been out in the sun a while. And this is Texas, right? Lots of sun. You can't just lie out in it like that."

"And you figured Supko would know that?"

"Oh yeah. That's…that's why I thought he was gone. To start with. Before we got him out of the pool." He ran his open palms up and down the air in front of his torso. "His skin. It's all red. Glowing." He wiped his open palm over the air in front of his face. "All red. His face. His lips. But one side of his face isn't burnt, right? Means he had been in the same position for a long time."

"Since ten thirty-seven in the morning, you mean?"

Barnes nodded. "But he had used some sunscreen."

Jess frowned. "Why do you think that?"

"His legs. His legs weren't too bad. Maybe a little red, but nothing like his face and arms, and, and all the top half of him. He's a real lobster."

"So he put some sunscreen on? That's odd, isn't it?"

"Puts it all over his legs then decides to kill himself?" He widened his eyes and lifted his hands, palms up. "Who puts sunscreen on if they're going to commit suicide?"

"Did you tell the police all this?"

"They said he could have just gone about his normal day, and then cracked. And they might be right." He shrugged. "Turns out his business was on the rocks."

"What business?"

"Some kind of finance thing. But he was only gone a couple of days and the bank repo'd his house. Took everything. House, contents, car. His missus? She had to leave. Got out just before the bank people arrived."

"Bet that was a scandal around here."

He guffawed. "Got that right. But, you know, most of them are up to their eyeballs, I'll bet."

Jess stepped back. Suicide or not, turned out Blazek had good reason to worry about Supko. His scheme had another victim. Or another culprit. Either way, Supko's business had bled dry like the forty-six other Blazek victims she'd interviewed.

Jess gripped her bag. "What happened to Mrs. Supko?"

Barnes seemed to think about the question a bit before gesturing to the young guard outside. "Jimmy, well...he probably knows. Takes her the mail a couple times a week. Ask him."

Jess glanced out the window toward Jimmy.

"I've got to get on, now." Barnes pulled a form from the rack on the wall. "Got an incident report to write."

# CHAPTER FIVE

JESS DROVE OUT OF Highland Village with Candace Supko's address wedged between the panels of her dashboard. Jimmy Polar had been hesitant to write it down. He'd owned up to taking her the mail because he lived nearby, but that was it. He claimed to know nothing else about the widow, but Jess didn't believe him.

She took Interstate 35 to 45 then onto 20, traveling in the right direction. She pulled into a gas station and typed the address into the GPS on her phone. She brought up a map and then an aerial satellite image of Candace Supko's new neighborhood.

She knew at once that the collapse of Joshua Supko's business had been complete. No grieving widow would willingly move her children from Highland Village to this neighborhood if she had any choice.

The GPS led her another three miles down the road and into an old mobile home park. The singlewides were lined up in precise rows. Some were freshly painted with neatly trimmed lawns. Others wore faded colors baked by the Texas sun and hadn't felt a brush of any kind in twenty years.

Two scrawny dogs and several well-fed feral cats roamed between sheds at the back of the lots. People dressed in sweat-stained tank tops and jeans worked in yards or sat on porches. Air-conditioning was probably a luxury many of these folks could not afford.

She pulled the Ford up to the address Polar had given her, and locked the car. For the second time in as many hours, her rental shouted its awkward pedigree, but this time because it looked too good for the neighborhood instead of too cheap.

On the drive, Jess had time to choose her approach to Mrs. Supko. She should have been the person most likely to know what was going on with her husband's business and life. Which made her an essential witness, but also might mean she'd be unwilling to talk about him to a reporter.

Candace Supko's new residence was one of the unpainted singlewides. A rusty white metal awning supported by rustier poles covered the concrete patio on the north side. Concrete steps led to the screen door. The lot was mostly dirt secured to the earth by weed patches here and there. Nothing resembling a plant or flower made any effort to improve the place.

Jess had interviewed too many widows in her career. Each had suffered pain and trouble. More often than not, they had fears, too. Pain and trouble often led a widow to talk freely, but fear always led to stony silence.

Jess walked carefully around the crevices and along the white-hot pavement the entire twenty feet from the car to the patio. The front screen door rattled in its frame as she knocked on it. After thirty seconds, she knocked again.

"Go away." A woman's voice traveled through the screen from the dark interior.

"Mrs. Supko? Candace Supko?"

"Go away."

"My name is Jess Kimball." She put friendly warmth into her tone. "I'd like to talk to you about your husband."

"Go away."

The heat under the awning at the front door was burned hotter than the bright sun by the car. Jess wiped the film of perspiration from above her lip. She could do nothing about the sweat trickling down inside her blouse. "I was very sorry to hear about his passing."

"Then go put flowers on his grave. Better still, give me the money." Mrs. Supko. Until now, Jess hadn't been sure.

"I think his death was…" She'd almost said not a suicide, but she caught herself. "Suspicious."

"No kidding." This time, Jess thought Mrs. Supko's speech was slurred. Maybe the woman had been drinking. Not that Jess would have blamed her.

Another trickle of sweat joined the last on its way down her side. Man, it was hot out here. "So, could we talk?"

"Just go away." Definitely a slur in there. Not sloppy, but not the way a sober woman speaks, either. "I've had enough of you do-gooders. All sweet and cuddly and totally useless."

*Ah.* So she'd been visited by child protective services, maybe a couple of charities, perhaps a few other agencies. Trying to help, for sure. But nothing they had to offer would restore this woman to her former life. "I'm not…I'm a reporter."

"Yeah, well. I've talked to enough of them, too."

"I'm with *Taboo Magazine.* Jessica Kimball." No response.

"Maybe you've read some of my victims' rights stories? I might be able to help you."

Jess listened to movement within. A creaking chair. Footsteps.

"We're a national—"

"I know what you are." The voice was closer. "How much?"

Jess sighed. Her curls adhered to the damp around the edges of her face. She blew a stream of air upward and wiped the sweat from her upper lip again. "You want me to pay you to talk?"

"Unless you have something else in mind?" Candace Supko had stopped short of the screen.

The interior was too dark to see her clearly. "Two hundred seems the going rate."

"For a national magazine?" Mrs. Supko's voice had regained its clarity. She lifted a glass filled with brown liquid to her mouth and swigged. "Pretty cheap."

"Four hundred." Jess dug into her wallet and showed the bills. "That's all I've got."

"One condition. You can write what you want about me, but leave my children out of it." Mrs. Supko came closer to see the money. "Not a word about my kids. You understand?"

"No problem." Jess held the bills out like bait.

"Promise?"

But Jess could see her eyes now. Shiny. Narrowed. Focused on the cash. Candace Supko was hooked like an addict needing a fix.

"I promise," Jess replied, feeling vaguely like she was the one who was taking instead of giving.

"Wait." Mrs. Supko shooed her children into one of the back rooms and then opened the door.

As soon as her eyes adjusted to the dim light inside, Jess

could see why Jimmy was so keen to bring her mail. Candace Supko had high cheekbones and skin that was warmed by the lightest of tans. Long blonde hair tumbled over her shoulders like a shampoo model. Even with her effort to appear disinterested, her rosy lips framed pearly whitened teeth with a near smile.

But Jimmy probably noticed none of these details. What he'd seen was Mrs. Supko's long legs extending well beyond the hem of the briefest of tan shorts and a close fitting pink t-shirt. She stood straight, muscles toned and trim by five-times-a-week Pilates, no doubt. Her figure was straight out of the specifications for bombshell.

She stepped to one side to allow Jess deeper access to her home, and closed the screen door behind her. "Sit down and let's get this over with."

The mobile home's main living area looked to be a single L-shaped room, two sofas and a tube television at one end, and a hallway that probably led to bedrooms in the back. In the center was a kitchenette. Jess presumed the bathroom nestled between the kitchenette and bedrooms filled out the L-shape into a square.

Jess sat on a sofa, sinking into its tired cushions with her knees crunched upwards. The walls were bare of all adornment except for a single framed piece in the center of the dark wood paneling that ran from the front to the back of the main room. Jess wouldn't have called it art, but someone must have liked it well enough to frame and hang.

Mrs. Supko took the other sofa and somehow managed to remain dignified. "I'd offer you coffee, but I don't have any."

"No problem."

Mrs. Supko held her hand out.

Jess pulled the money from her wallet, and handed over roughly half. "The rest if you can answer a few questions, Mrs. Supko."

"Call me Candace." She counted the money. "Two forty. Not that I don't trust you, but my children need to eat." She tucked the money into her pocket. "What's your angle?"

"On your husband?" Jess parted her lips and breathed through her mouth. The combined odor of hot humans and stale air was revolting.

"On whatever you're writing in your article," Candace Supko said.

Jess nodded. "The article is coming together. But for this section, I'm interested in your late husband."

"Josh was a good guy." She flashed a flat smile. "No matter what happened, and I don't pretend to understand it all, he was a good guy."

"How did you meet?"

"Society do. Charity thing." She laughed. A cute happy laugh. The sort of thing television shows dubbed onto sitcoms. "Buy a thousand-dollar ticket, dress up like the ticket was nothing, and meet a bunch of rich guys with no one to spend their money on."

Jess smiled.

"Don't kid yourself that you're better than me, Miss Kimball." Mrs. Supko's mirth evaporated.

Jess shook her head. "Candace, I wasn't—"

"We've all got to use our gifts to get through life. You're an intellectual." She ran her palms over her hips and smiled again. "I'm better in the physical department. No offense intended."

"Actually, I was wishing I'd thought of the idea." Jess

dipped her chin and cleared her throat. "So, what happened after you met?"

"There was fifteen years between us. Most people would see that as terminal in a relationship, but," Candace Supko shrugged, "turns out we were perfect for each other. He's into finance. Wants to look good. Impress people. Make people like him."

Jess raised her eyebrows and cocked her head. *Keep talking.*

Mrs. Supko took another sip. Her tongue flicked out to lick her lips. "Easy to do when almost everyone he wanted to impress was male."

Jess nodded slowly. Now that she'd started talking, Candace Supko warmed to her subject and Jess didn't want to interrupt the flow.

"I know what you're thinking, and yes, I was his trophy wife. But he was my trophy, too. My ticket." Mrs. Supko bobbed her head up, gazing directly at Jess. "See, I grew up near here. Four kids. Place like this. Never a moment's privacy. I don't regret it. I love my family. I just didn't want to live all my life like," she waved her arm to encompass the entire room, "like this."

"So, you married him." Jess heard the disapproval in her own voice. Candace probably did, too.

"Of course. I'd made it. All I had to do was keep it going. Which I did." She arched her perfectly arched eyebrows and pouted a bit. "Don't think it's easy. I had a full-time job keeping it all together. Small talk at business dinners. Receptions by the pool. Social circles. The kids. The whole ball of wax."

"I see," Jess said because it seemed Candace expected Jess's approval every now and then.

"I worked hard at our relationship. He did, too." Her voice softened. She pinched the hems of her shorts with her fingers. "Josh was remarkably faithful. I had him followed from time to time, and nothing. He was a financial geek. Stayed in his hotel room working late into the night. No hanging out at the bar, hoping to get lucky."

Jess nodded.

"Whenever we weren't together, he was hunched over his desk, figuring out how to make us richer. How many women can say that?" Mrs. Supko's expression was defiant.

Jess bit her lip. The question wasn't meant to be answered. "Until two months ago."

Candace exhaled slowly. Her face seemed a shade whiter. She nodded.

Jess waited a few moments before speaking. "Can you tell me about that day? What happened?"

She took a deep breath, folded her hands, and spoke without inflection, as if she'd told the story many times before, which she surely had. "Kitty…well, a friend was having a birthday party for her son. Big affair. I went over earlier that morning to help set up for the afternoon party. Took my two with me. They had, like, fifty guests." She drew another long breath, inhaling through her nose. "I didn't see Josh till we got home. Brought some of the neighbor's kids back with me. Give Kitty a break, time to straighten her house. You know."

She paused, inhaled again. She winced. "And there he was. Lying on the lounger. In the pool. I…" She opened and closed her mouth twice before she pushed the next words out. "…thought he'd had a heart attack. I jumped in the water, and…" She halted and then breathed a few times. She blinked away the glassy tears in her eyes. "You know, you don't have to be a doctor to know when someone's dead."

Another long pause while she sipped to cover her emotions, but Jess simply waited.

"I got out. Ran for the button. Big red panic button by the door. To...to call security. Then I put the kids in the front room. Shut the door. They'd seen him, of course." She shook her head and squeezed her eyes closed a couple of moments. "It wasn't...I didn't know... They were asking questions, talking, crying. I didn't know what to say." She shook her head again, slower and harder this time. "I couldn't even speak."

Jess leaned forward, her hand out as if for comfort even though she couldn't reach across the divide. "I'm sorry."

Candace Supko looked at the outstretched hand, her lips pressed firmly together, and lifted her head. "Yeah. Well. Not the sort of thing you can just fix, is it?"

"No." Jess shook her head slowly and withdrew her hand. So many things in life couldn't be fixed. Jess knew that as well as anyone. "What about the police?"

The bleak look in her eyes gave Jess the feeling that Candace Supko walked a thin line between control and total breakdown every minute of every day. The woman had to be completely terrified.

"Yeah. They turned up." She squared her shoulders and took another steadying breath. "And security, and the fire people, and an ambulance. It was a madhouse. All those people. Something about the housing association rules."

"What did they find?"

Candace raised her eyebrows.

Jess said, "The police. At the scene."

She shrugged and looked away. "Josh, obviously. There wasn't much else to find. When you've got a dead body in your pool, everything else is pretty much—"

"Did they know it was cyanide?"

Candace shook her head and chewed the inside of her cheek.

"That was a few days later. Autopsy."

"Did they find any signs of cyanide at the house?"

"You mean, did I do it? Did I have a stash under—"

"No. Not at all." Jess held her hand up. "I meant, did they find any around the pool while they were there?"

Candace stared straight ahead, vacantly, emotionless. "They said he must have taken it all. Several tablets, apparently. From his blood tests."

"Do you believe that?"

She shrugged. "I don't think there's any doubt he died of cyanide poisoning."

"I meant, do you believe he committed suicide?" Jess frowned.

"Miss Kimball, Josh was a lot of things. And yes, he was worried. But he was often worried. One time he gambled our house, hocked it, and for twenty-four hours, it looked like he'd lost it." She squared her shoulders and filled her lungs. "So, sure. He was worried, but he wasn't suicidal. Not in the slightest. You live with someone for twelve years, and you get to know these things."

Jess leaned in, as if being physically closer to his widow would bring Jess closer to the truth about his death, too. "But the police believe it was suicide."

"They didn't know Josh. All they focused on was that his business collapsed." Candace sipped the last of her drink and set the glass down on the table next to her chair. "He was tapped out. I didn't know. No clue. Nada. He'd bet the house again. Mortgaged everything away."

Jess thought about the logistics for a moment before she asked, "Did he leave a note?"

Candace shook her head.

"A will?"

"He left me all the debts. But I'll get back up again."

"What about his business associates?"

Her eyebrows arched and her lips formed a little O of surprise. "You mean, will they help me?"

"Sorry. I meant, who was he working with at the time?"

Candace shrugged. "Bunch of people really. They were the latest big thing. But he had others. Lots of others. I never really kept track of the names."

"Did any of them come to the house?"

"Not that I saw. They used to. After the children were born, he started meeting people in other places."

"Do you have his business papers?"

"The police took everything first and then the bank took it all. Perhaps I should have hung on to things, but it's hard to tell the bank no when you're hoping they'll forgive the debt on your home."

Jess considered how much to reveal. "Did he ever mention the name Blazek?"

"Marek?"

"No, Blazek."

Candace pouched her lips and shook her head.

"Warga, Zmich, Grantly?"

She shook her head again. "Maybe Grantly, but it's a common name. I'm not sure. Why?"

"I think they might be connected."

"To what?"

"You haven't heard of Blazek? He's been on the news."

"That guy?" Mrs. Supko snorted. "He's a con artist. Josh wasn't a con artist. He was good with finance. Risk mitigation. Futures. He made us money and he made other people money.

He was good with investments."

"What did he invest in?"

"What didn't he invest in? Gold, oil, wool, new road construction, paintings, buildings. Everything was fair game if he could see a way to a profit. He was good at it. Consistent. Even with the art, and believe me, love him as I did, he had no eye for art."

*Interesting list.* "What art?"

"Paintings. Never anything else. He'd go for new artists. Unknowns. Snap them up and sell them a few months later." Candace collected her glass and walked to the kitchen. She pulled the whiskey bottle down from a high shelf and tilted it toward Jess.

"No, thanks. I'm driving."

"Suit yourself. The ones that didn't sell easily ended up on our walls. We'd laugh at them sometimes." Candace poured three fingers of whiskey into her glass and added a splash of tap water. She took a sip to judge the mix and turned to lean against the counter. "Hell, some of those things were crap. The kids could do better. But eventually they'd sell. He'd turn a profit and move on to the next."

"Always a profit? Never a loss?"

"Win some lose some. That's investment, he'd say." She swigged a large mouthful of the whiskey and coughed a little as it burned down her throat. "He kept on buying them. Every couple of months."

"Where did he buy the art?"

"There's always private sales going on." Candace tipped her glass to the framed painting on the wall Jess had noticed earlier. "Like that piece of crap there. I brought it with me because even the bank didn't want it when they foreclosed. Aside from the kids, it's the only thing I have left that belonged to Josh."

Jess pushed herself out of the soft cushions and walked to the painting for a closer inspection. The gilded frame suggested a grandiose masterpiece. The image was not much more than swipes of color applied with a wide brush moving from bottom left to top right. If the swipes had been arched and the colors not quite as vivid, the color band would have resembled a child's rainbow. The painting was signed by an artist Jess had never heard of, I.M. Zimmer.

She pulled her phone from her pocket and took a couple of quick snaps of the painting. Candace didn't object.

"He sold the art in private sales, too?" Jess returned to the couch and fell into its too soft depths again.

Candace nodded. "No commissions that way, he said."

"So, no taxes either?"

"I never got into that. Even if he didn't pay taxes on them, I have nothing left to give. So you won't get much out of reporting me."

"I have less love for the IRS than most Americans. Don't worry." Jess cocked her head. "Why didn't you push your doubts about the suicide theory with the police?"

"By the time that was coming out, I was looking at places like this to find a place for my kids to sleep, and believe me, this was the best I could find. So, my voice didn't count much with the cops. They figured I was trailer trash and we don't get as much respect as Highland Village. Not even close." She swigged again and coughed it down. "That housing association chairwoman's a bitch, too. She'd shoot the president if she thought it would keep her housing values up. She wanted the case closed and that was that."

Her suspicions didn't make much sense to Jess and she

shook her head. "A housing association can't influence a police investigation."

Candace laughed. "You went over to our old house, didn't you? Jimmy told me. See what happened? Security right there in two shakes of an armadillo's tail. That place is tied up tighter than a duck's…"

Jess smiled. "Are you and Jimmy…" She let her voice trail.

"Are we what, Miss Kimball?" She leaned forward. "He's an all muscle, two hundred-pound security guard who, as you can see from his face, isn't the kind to back down. He comes round here in his uniform with a gun on his hip." She nodded out of the window. "Did you look around when you arrived? How safe do you think I'd be here as a single girl? So, every time he turns up I roll out the welcome mat. I go out there where the neighbors can see. Hug him. Smile. Laugh. Hold his hand, and drag him in here."

Jess nodded, chewing on her lower lip. "I understand."

"No you don't. I'm no tramp, so don't go writing me up like that. He brings coffee, and we just talk. Besides," she gestured to the back bedrooms where the kids were playing, "I have the best contraceptive you can get."

Jess cocked her head.

Candace smiled. "You don't have kids, do you?"

"I…" Jess looked down. "No."

Supko's smile faded and she didn't press. "Jimmy told me you wanted to see Josh. Tell him he was in danger."

"Blazek told me he was worried for your husband. He implied they were in business together."

Candace shook her head. "He never mentioned Blazek, and I told you, Josh was no con artist."

"But your husband may have been murdered."

Mrs. Supko took a deep breath and let it out slowly. "Do you think I should worry? My kids?"

Jess frowned. "It's been two months since…since your husband died. If anything was going to happen, I think it would have by now."

Candace tapped the whiskey glass on her front teeth.

"Either way, you might want to keep Jimmy interested till you can afford another thousand-dollar event ticket." Jess handed over the remainder of the money she'd promised for the interview. Candace Supko's hand shot out to collect the bills and stuff them in her pocket as if Jess might change her mind.

# CHAPTER SIX

JESS DROVE THE FORD along the path around the park, and waited behind a 1970s era pickup truck to join the main road, deep in thought.

For a woman who had recently lost her husband, Candace Supko seemed very much in control of her emotions. She was cool and calculating, yet down-to-earth. The fall from conspicuous wealth into the poverty trap had left her confident and determined. Her honesty was refreshing. In happier circumstances, Jess guessed she'd been a popular neighbor at Highland Village.

The battered green pickup truck inched forward for a better view of oncoming traffic.

Jess tapped her fingertips on the steering wheel. Candace Supko and her husband had been a good match, she'd said. Josh Supko had probably been determined, cool, and confident, too. She said he hadn't displayed the typical despair of a man driven to the end of his rope. Or one likely to swallow cyanide and die splayed out on a lounger in full view of his kids.

The more Jess learned about Josh Supko, the less likely suicide seemed.

The pickup pulled out, leaving a cloud of blue smoke behind. Jess stabbed the recirculate button, but the gag-inducing smell of half-burnt hydrocarbons filled the Ford. She pulled up to the stop sign, waited for a gap, and followed the pickup truck's smoke toward Dallas.

If Josh Supko hadn't killed himself, then his death was a homicide. Which presented a whole new barrage of questions. Who killed him?

Blazek's story that he was "worried" about Josh Supko was another in his long string of lies. He must have known Supko was dead. But he probably didn't kill Supko.

At the time of death, Blazek was enjoying free food and television courtesy of the Texas Department of Criminal Justice. And if he'd hired Supko's killer, why send Jess to uncover that fact when Supko's death had been ruled a suicide and Blazek was already free of suspicion?

No. Supko's killer was probably not Blazek.

In most murder investigations, the spouse was a prime suspect. Money, love, jealousy, the stress of daily existence under one roof. All of that could drive lovers over the edge. Candace Supko seemed almost clinically cool about her husband's death, but that wasn't evidence that she'd killed him.

What possible motive did she have?

Jess bit her lip. No matter what qualities Jimmy the security guard might possess, Candace Supko wasn't likely to give up Highland Village for mere lust. She was too cool for that.

The pickup truck finally turned right, taking its smoky tailpipe with it. Jess opened the vents and lowered the front windows to freshen the air inside the Ford. She pushed the cruise control up another five miles an hour.

What about money? Candace Supko didn't appear to know much about her husband's investments, or lack of them, until after he died. Maybe she had believed she would be rich when Josh died and got impatient. Women had made that choice before.

That answer didn't feel right, though. Candace Supko hadn't seemed angry with her husband for leaving her penniless with mouths to feed and no means to do so. She'd accepted her changed circumstances and already had a plan in place to find another trophy husband.

Which left Jess with her least favorite option. Blazek's mysterious international crime ring, the Italians. She snorted. The idea seemed as preposterous now as it had when Blazek first mentioned it.

She took the entrance ramp for I-20 west, and settled into the middle lane, still running ten miles an hour above the speed limit.

Candace Supko had been right about one thing, that gated community was tied up tight. They had cameras everywhere. They would have a record of everyone who'd entered and exited the estate. Jess considered driving back to Highland Village to check out the security guard's backseat passenger.

The police would have taken the recordings, though. They would have pored over the videos. She wouldn't find a man traveling in the backseat of a BMW if the forensics teams hadn't seen him.

She turned onto I-45 toward Dallas and checked the clock. Plenty of time before her flight.

The other names on Blazek's list of friends might be worth

checking, but she needed to talk to one more person in Dallas before she decided to track them down.

Jess switched on the car's phone, waited for the Bluetooth to sync up with her phone, and voice-dialed a number from her address book. The number rang five times before he answered.

"Special Agent Henry Morris." His voice was gruff, rushed.

"Agent Morris, Jessica Kimball. I wonder if I could have a moment of your time?"

He paused, perhaps to check his watch. "Go ahead."

"In person."

Morris took a deep breath. "In conjunction with what?"

"Stosh Blazek."

"Nothing to talk about. He pled guilty. Last-minute plea bargain, I'm told. He's going to jail. Score one for the good guys."

Jess ran open fingers through her hair. "He gave me some names, and...can't I buy you a coffee?"

"Look, I'm busy. I can't waste time helping you to fill out your story for your magazine. Sorry if that sounds curt, but I have more than enough to do."

"I think I have some new information."

Morris was silent.

"I won't take long. I've got new information you'll want to hear and I don't want to talk about it on an open phone line." Jess knew how to persuade busy people to make time for her. She'd had loads of practice. "I'll buy lunch. You need to eat, don't you?"

"You need a dictionary. Look up the word 'no'." Morris groaned before he gave in. "You know Café Bistro? In front of our building?"

"I can be there in thirty minutes."

"There and then."

"See—" Jess closed her mouth. Morris had already hung up. She had half an hour to figure out how to persuade him to help her.

# CHAPTER SEVEN

*Dallas, Texas*
*May 10*

JESS HAD WORKED WITH many detectives in the years since her son was stolen, and she'd learned to instantly identify the ones she could rely on. Henry Morris was one of those.

He'd been an FBI Special Agent for ten years. Energetic. Well regarded. Upwardly mobile. The Stosh Blazek story had garnered a fair amount of local publicity for him in Dallas and he'd come off well in the press.

He'd been helpful to her before, which was always a good indicator in her book.

Morris was destined for a starring role in the FBI one day if he stayed on the side of the angels instead of falling for all that protect-the-criminal crap. In her two previous phone calls with the man, he'd seemed like a guy looking to score a big take down, and she hoped he'd be as angry about Blazek's plea deal as she was. Angry enough to reopen the case.

There was another good reason to meet with him. He was an

ideal focal point for her *Taboo* feature. She often skewered law and justice, which weren't even close to the same thing. Featuring a strong cop helped her readers realize that even though the system often failed, sometimes justice *was* served.

Jess entered the busy coffee bar. A sea of dark suits defined the place as a hangout for cops and lawyers. Not surprising since Café Bistro sat squarely across the street from One Justice Way, the building that housed the FBI's Dallas Field Office. Problem was she'd never seen Morris, and she was looking at rows of square shoulders, cheap dark suits, and boring haircuts.

She pressed the redial button on her phone. The call rang through and she scanned the crowd. The man in the back corner answered it on the third ring.

"Morris with your coffee," he said, the voice in her ear confirming the guess she'd made about his identity.

"Kimball at three o'clock."

"I know." His gaze met hers and he disconnected the call.

She threaded her way through the crowded tables to reach him.

He didn't stand, but extended his hand. He had a firm grip. Another good sign. Jess wasn't wimpy and she didn't like her detectives wimpy, either.

Not too handsome, but not too bad. Dark hair, dark eyes, and a scar that slashed his lip on the left side. That, and a nose that had been broken more than once, made his face more interesting than it might otherwise have been. He was an active cop and he didn't always win, but she'd bet the other guy had always looked worse.

Morris wore a plain gold band on his left ring finger. Jess made a mental note. Married usually meant more careful, which was a good thing. The last thing she wanted was a Texas Cowboy she had to manage.

"Sorry." She looked around to check the level of privacy they'd have here. "I didn't recognize you."

He smiled and held up a month-old copy of *Taboo Magazine*. Her picture was displayed beside her bio at the bottom of the page. "I had the advantage."

She settled into the chair across the table from him. "I didn't know you were a subscriber."

He put the magazine down between them. "I'm not. My dentist, on the other hand..."

She laughed. "You stole it?"

"I'm a regular visitor, and at the prices he charges, he can afford a copy or two."

"Nothing serious, I hope?"

"An ounce of prevention." He flashed his teeth as if showing his mom he'd brushed before bedtime. "The FBI, remember? We get good medical benefits."

She grinned. "Right." Her instincts were right about this guy.

The noise in the café was too loud for her recorder. She pulled out a notebook and pen to take down quotes. "Thanks for sparing me some time. I was trying to put a wrap on the Blazek case."

"Case? I thought you wrote lifestyle magazine articles."

She grimaced. "Not exactly. *Taboo* is a lifestyle magazine, but my articles aren't about fashion and food. Crime is my beat and my focus is on victims' rights."

"Not a defender of the Constitution, then?"

"Victims have Constitutional rights, too, don't they? What about life, liberty, and the pursuit of happiness?" Jess inhaled slowly to control her temper. She'd get nowhere with this guy if she pissed him off right at the start. "I want a level playing field. I want the Constitution to work the way it should. What about you?"

He nodded slowly as if he was sizing her up, which he probably was. "What did you think of Blazek when you talked to him?"

She frowned.

Morris nodded again. "Until he's formally handed over to the Department of Criminal Justice for prison, I get notified about everyone who talks to him."

He was judging her, so she chose her words precisely and for impact. "He is an obvious sociopath. No conscience at all. Lives in a fantasy land where everything is being done to him, not the other way around. Not even a smidgen of personal responsibility."

"Uh-huh."

"He's a liar."

"Pathological."

"Right. But even though he's the kind of guy who would prey on anyone weaker than him, he doesn't seem the type to have fallen for an advance fee scam."

He nodded approval, as if she was a particularly apt pupil. "He's not."

Jess stifled her indignation and continued. "Which means these scammers are better than most. Probably good in the early and middle phases of the con. Since Blazek claims he pled guilty to avoid them, I guess they are worse than most on the back end."

Maybe she'd passed whatever test he'd devised because Morris leaned back in his chair. He slouched, hands in his pockets. "You've seen the court file?"

"Nothing remarkable about the initial pitch Blazek received. It's a classic opener for this type of con." She noticed the room's reduced background noise. She glanced into the round mirror mounted on the wall above Morris's head. Café Bistro patrons came and went through the front door, but the total body count seemed lower.

"Yep." He sounded almost friendly now.

"What made the pitch an offer a guy like Blazek couldn't refuse?"

Morris extended his legs and crossed his feet at the ankles. "Most of these scammers are small time operators, sending out thousands of pitches every day all over the world. They expect a miniscule return rate."

Her radar relaxed. She read his friendly tone and offer of a few facts as a sign that she'd run the gauntlet and emerged somehow as worthy. "Everybody gets them. They are obvious fakes to anybody with a little business savvy, like Blazek."

"But these guys are another breed of cat altogether." He reached for his cup and sipped his coffee.

She picked her coffee up and sipped, too, acting interested like a colleague would. "How so?"

"The initial hook was clever in four important ways." He held out his fingers to count them off. "One, the pitch came by certified mail. Two, it was addressed to Stosh Blazek, *Esquire*, meaning they knew he was a lawyer. And three, his personal signature was required to claim the certified mail. A signature by a secretary or a colleague wouldn't suffice."

"A lawyer would notice anything that required his personal signature. He'd think it was personal, meant for him only. And sending it certified gave the original package a degree of traceability, too. So, it seemed more legitimate and enticing."

Jess knew all of this, but he was probably going somewhere with the background. Now that she had him talking, she wanted to keep the words flowing, too.

"Even though it can be faked."

"Okay." She nodded. "What was the fourth point?"

Morris used his thumb instead of his pinky to mark the last item. "The most important point. The letter claimed one of his law school classmates recommended him. A guy named Aleksy Kowalski in New Orleans."

Tiny hairs stood up on the back of Jess's neck. She felt the familiar electricity that always warned her when she was on the right track. Aleksy Kowalski was one of the names on the list Blazek had given her at the jail.

"Not exactly a name a scammer might pull out of thin air, is it?" she said.

Morris quickly stifled the grin that lifted his lips at the corner. "Not only that, Blazek and Kowalski had referred business to each other in the past, though Blazek said the pair hadn't seen each other in years."

"But a savvy guy like Blazek wouldn't have been sucked in, even by the seemingly legitimate letter. Wouldn't he have checked with Kowalski before he got involved?"

"He claimed he called and Kowalski vouched for the deal." Morris leaned forward, hands folded around his coffee, elbows resting on the table. "That's where things got more interesting. We found no evidence of that call."

The reason was obvious, but she chewed her lip a moment like she was thinking things through. "Because the call was never made."

"That." Morris was skilled at interview techniques. He'd led her to the question and next he'd supply a better answer. "And because we couldn't find Kowalski."

"He doesn't exist?"

"Oh, Kowalski exists. Or he did at one time, anyway."

Morris seemed to warm to his subject. He leaned in further. "We found his house in the Garden District in New Orleans, but we can't find him now and we spent a fair amount of time looking."

"Why didn't you tell Blazek?"

"I did. Blazek knows."

She frowned again. So Blazek lied about Morris failing to follow up on his claims, too. She wasn't surprised. Blazek wouldn't know the truth if it bit him in the ass.

Morris grunted, a sound something like laughter. "Blazek claims otherwise, doesn't he? Spent all his time crying on your shoulder about how the FBI was ignoring his legitimate defenses and not making any effort to find the real bad guys, right? That guy's nose is longer than Pinocchio's."

A quick laugh escaped Jess's throat at the mental image, although Blazek was more like a crazy killer in a horror movie to her than the charming wooden boy with a penchant for harmless lies. "Something like that. He gave me five names."

"Let me guess. Kowalski, Warga, Supko, Zmich, and Grantly."

"Odd names." She finished her coffee and wiggled a little, fruitlessly seeking a more comfortable position on the hard chair.

"My boss thinks Warga and Zmich are from New York." He shrugged and leaned back. "But then, he thinks everyone with an unusual name is from New York. He doesn't trust the place."

"Blazek said they were all victims, and you did nothing to help them."

"Oh yeah, *victims*. That's rich. They're thieves. Like Blazek." His mouth formed a hard line. After a moment's pause, he said, "Grantly is the odd man out. He has a thriving real estate business in Florida. We talked to him. Said he didn't need any help, and wasn't involved. We searched his phone and bank records. He hadn't connected with Blazek in over four years."

"So, Grantly's off the list." Jess watched his face for micro expressions to prove he was being less than truthful with her, but she saw none. Her gut said she could trust him. Then again, she'd been wrong before.

Morris's lips pressed tight and his gaze pierced straight through her as if he could see the quality of her heart. One of them would have to take a chance.

Jess opened her mouth to ask him what he was thinking, but he cut her off. "Advanced fee scammers have come a long way from the old Nigerian letter fraud. These days they operate the world over. Most are small potatoes, hoping for a score. But some are a lot more expert."

She had already researched Blazek's scam. It was distressingly familiar because it worked far too often to steal the lives of victims.

In the old days, the scammer would collect money from a series of progressively more profitable contacts with a single person. They worked on a volume basis. They sent thousands of invitations and hit the jackpot less than one percent of the time, like any direct-mail marketer.

When they found a good prospect, they would persuade the victim to pay a fee in advance of some promised windfall. The windfall was always framed as a request for help and an offer to pay for that help with an outrageously huge sum of money way too good to be true. Which was the first hint that the scammer was playing the victim for a sucker.

Once the gullible victim fell under the scammer's spell, the scammer would keep asking for "fees," money for this and that, always leading toward the promised millions of dollars, but never quite getting there.

Eventually, the victim would give up.

Some would climb into high-dollar levels before they figured out they were being scammed, but most did not.

They'd wise up, or run out of money, and that was the end. The scammer moved on. The victim was left in a world of hurt.

The scams weren't reported because the victims were either too embarrassed or felt guilty. In some cases, the victims had become criminals themselves because they embezzled money to pay the scammers and were now in too deep.

For the scammer, the victim was nothing but a hit and run. The scammer found a new batch of email addresses that would lead them to the next victim. The scammer was long gone.

Jess squared her shoulders. "You think Kowalski was running the scam, using Blazek and the others? Kowalski folded his tent and disappeared because Blazek got caught?"

"Could be. Scammers work better in teams. They prop each other up, and give the illusion of respectability."

The café's espresso machine gurgled and hissed. Coffee aroma filled the air. Her stomach gurgled like the machine. She sniffed the dregs in her cup and placed it back on the table, regretting she hadn't finished it while it was hot.

"You said you had some new information for me."

She pushed the cup aside and folded her hands on the table. "I went to see Joshua Supko."

"Ah."

"He's dead."

"One of the few definite facts in this whole affair." He shrugged.

"Right. Sorry." She nodded. "Stupid of me to think you might not know already."

"Was Supko's death what you wanted to tell me about?"

"Not exactly. Do you buy the suicide story?"

"Do you?"

She shook her head. "He was a successful businessman. At least that's what his wife thinks."

"You met her?"

"Yes. She's gone down in the world."

"I have the feeling she'll get back up. She has…assets." Jess grinned.

"Don't get me wrong." He held up his wedding band and wiggled his fingers. "She's a fighter and a survivor."

"She said she and her husband were a good match. So, was he a fighter and a survivor?"

"Apparently. Up until the last."

"Why was his death determined a suicide?"

"If we had any evidence to the contrary, it wouldn't be."

"That's the problem with this whole Blazek affair, isn't it?"

"Why yes, Miss Kimball, yes it is." He picked up her cup. "Perhaps I should buy lunch."

She watched while he approached the counter and stood in line. In her experience, the FBI expected citizens to cooperate with them. They only bought lunch for their wives and informants, and she wasn't his wife.

So, he was hoping she would have or find some evidence against Blazek and his friends. Something the FBI hadn't been able to find. Hard facts that would capture the rest of Blazek's ring and maybe result in new charges against Blazek, too. Bring them all down. Give the victims at least a small measure of justice.

She took a deep breath. All of that was more than fine with her. She had been looking forward to a few days off to recharge her batteries starting tomorrow. But she couldn't leave this job unfinished, even if it seemed the FBI could.

She'd be doing the work either way. She might as well get some help from the FBI while she chased the facts.

She could do things the FBI couldn't, and the other way around, too. For this job, Morris and Kimball could be a good team.

Maybe.

Morris returned with a tray of two steaming espressos and four small cellophane wrapped blueberry muffins. "Best they've got left up there I'm afraid."

Jess didn't wait to be asked. She took a shot of the espresso, and started on one of the muffins. She spoke with her mouth half full. "Do you think Blazek was at the top of the tree on this team?"

He curled up one side of his face and swallowed the muffin. "Possibly, I suppose."

"Because that's all the evidence you were able to find?"

"Blazek has been convicted. He's made partial restitution to his victims, and he's on his way to federal prison. Case closed as far as my bosses are concerned." He popped the rest of the muffin into his mouth.

She picked up her espresso. "What about the rest of the group?"

"We're a part of the government. It's all about doing the best for the masses. Biggest bang for the public buck. And believe me when I tell you, we've got a boat load of other cases." He waved his hand toward the FBI building. "I've got seven active cases that I'm working on right this minute. All important. It's like whack-a-mole. We just hit the one standing highest, and move on to the next."

"Like Blazek and his scammers. You gave him a good

whack and can't take the time to finish the job."

He glowered, but she sensed he was angry with the situation and she'd found the real reason he'd agreed to meet with her.

She put her cup back on the table. "I just meant—"

"I know. Thing is, I can't follow up. There's a hundred loose ends and—"

"Do you trust me?" She put every ounce of sincerity she could muster into the question because FBI agents score off the charts on skepticism in personality tests. If he didn't trust her, this conversation had been a total waste of time.

Morris leaned back as if she was invading his personal comfort zone. "What does trust have to do with anything?"

"Because the only important thing in your Blazek investigation right now is information. And when the FBI shares information, you have to trust the person you're giving it to."

He shrugged. "The Blazek case is over. Everything we have is now a matter of public record."

She narrowed her eyes and shook her head slowly. "Not everything, Agent Morris. You never release everything. You don't have to release everything and you might need some of that seemingly unessential stuff in the future. You've held things back."

"True. But you could spend a week picking through the public leftovers and know just as much as I do. Maybe more."

"Suppose I do that."

He produced a silver flash drive from his pocket. "Suppose you did. Suppose you dug into all the bits and pieces we found and didn't use. Suppose you collected all of it onto this." He turned the flash drive over in his fingers. "You could have. Then you'd have a lot of stuff to go on."

She stared at the drive, willing him to hand it over. "You want me to investigate."

He nodded. "And to publicize. To dig stuff up. Jog memories. Give other victims courage."

"To find evidence."

He leaned forward. "Just point us to it, Jess. We'll enforce the law, and handle the justice. We'd do it ourselves if we could. It's not for a lack of desire, it's pure workload."

"Whack-a-mole."

He nodded and held out his palm.

She wrapped her fingers around the drive.

"There are a couple of things I should tell you," he said.

She put the drive in her pocket, and cleared her throat.

"You found Supko was dead." He nodded to her pocket. "So are Warga and Zmich. All suicides."

Jess's eyes widened. "Cyanide?"

He scowled and didn't reply.

"How can you not follow up on this?"

"This is bad, Jess. But we've got other cases that are worse. A lot worse." He took a deep breath. "If you saw what we're dealing with, maybe you'd understand."

Her nostrils flared and she felt her heart thumping hard. She breathed in through her nose, and back out again. Slowly. She was overreacting. She knew it. He'd handed her what could have taken her weeks to find. He was boxed into a corner, and she'd offered him an option. He wasn't ignoring the Blazek scammers. He was taking a leap of faith, depending on her.

She took another breath and another and another until she could speak calmly again. "Why were the deaths determined as suicides?"

Morris glanced at his watch. He answered her questions quickly. "They all occurred in different states, and at the time, we didn't have the link between the names."

"But cyanide?"

"Not that rare, unfortunately. It's not hard to obtain." He waved his hand. "Cyanide is used in several industries, and there are places on the Internet to buy it in large quantities."

"What about the other two, Kowalski and Grantly?"

"We can't find Kowalski. Grantly says he's healthy, wealthy, and not involved."

"So, if they are part of his team and still out there scamming, why did Blazek identify them?"

"Good question."

"Is Blazek a suspect?"

"For the suicides? Warga and Zmich, maybe. Not for Supko. Blazek was in custody by then."

"And you've no idea where Kowalski is? None?"

Morris shook his head twice, fast and hard.

"If we could connect Blazek—"

"We didn't charge him with murder. So he can't claim double jeopardy." Morris nodded as if she'd located the chink in Blazek's armor.

"But it would mean they committed three murders, for sure. Supko, Warga, and Zmich."

He nodded again.

"Which leaves us with Kowalski or Grantly as the only two left on the inside of the team."

"And Kowalski has disappeared."

"He's in hiding?"

"We think so. Yes. From us or from the other murderer."

Jess exhaled. "Too many options."

Morris grunted another of his humorless laughs. "Exactly what my boss said. Right before he directed me to my never-ending supply of other cases." He pulled a post-it from his pocket. "Last known addresses. For Kowalski and Grantly. If you're interested."

She took the note, flipping it between her fingers. "Mrs. Supko mentioned another name. Mark or Mar-zeck or something. It kind of rhymed with Blazek."

"What did she say?"

"Nothing. She just confused the two names."

"Mar-zeck and Blazek?"

Jess nodded.

Morris thought for a moment. "New one on me."

"We were talking about who her husband had been working with."

Morris shrugged. "Add him to the list. Just don't tell my boss."

"I don't think I want to meet your boss."

Morris shook his head. "He's trying to do the best job with too few resources, that's all." His eyebrows knitted together. "I've read your bio, Jess. What was it you said? There's no justice when the victims have no chance to be made whole? Well, we don't even know all the victims in Blazek's scheme, let alone the criminals, but that doesn't stop us from trying to do our jobs."

"You mean it doesn't stop me from trying, don't you?"

"I have every faith." Morris gave her a genuine smile that flashed most of his recently cleaned teeth. "But these men are dangerous, Jess. If we're right, they're cold-blooded killers. So stay inside the lines this time, okay?"

She didn't reply.

Morris placed a heavy hand on her forearm and looked straight into her eyes. "I won't be able to help you if you go off the reservation on this, Jess. Stick to the rules and we'll all be fine."

# CHAPTER EIGHT

MORRIS SHOOK HANDS OUTSIDE the coffee shop, and headed back into the FBI building.

Jess walked to her car. Five men on Blazek's list. Kowalski, Warga, Zmich, Supko, and Grantly. Three suicides. One missing. One claimed to be uninvolved.

Could Blazek be at the center of that team?

What about Kowalski? Had he killed the others and bugged out? Had he set up shop somewhere else already?

She unlocked her car and settled into a bubble of hot, sticky air. It made sense that he'd relocated only if Kowalski thought his guilt would be discovered. She started the engine, flipped the air-conditioner to full, and turned the vents to blast cold air on her face.

Morris would have checked airline records, so Kowalski couldn't simply have hopped on a plane, murdered Supko and the others and flown home. New Orleans to Dallas was a long drive, and Morris would have checked credit card activity that might have revealed a road trip.

Jess turned the Kowalski problem over in her mind a bit longer but nothing brilliant popped up.

Which left Grantly, the real estate guy from Florida. She rummaged in her bag and found Morris's post it note. New Orleans for Kowalski or Florida for Grantly? Neither option caused the familiar frissons along her spine that usually suggested one choice was better than the other. Tossing a coin seemed like a reasonable option here.

Like Morris's boss, she had to go where she stood the greatest chance of finding something, the biggest potential bang for her buck. Kowalski had disappeared. He seemed a more likely killer than Grantly. If she could find him, or find out something from his friends, neighbors, or co-workers that Morris hadn't found, then the FBI might put more resources on the case.

And New Orleans was on the way to Florida. Sort of.

She pulled out her phone and called her editor's assistant.

Mandy Donovan's voice mail kicked in and Jess smiled. She was a delightful person, but Jess didn't have the energy for her endless stream of small talk. "Mandy, it's Jess. I need a seat on the next flight from Dallas to New Orleans. I'll need a hotel and a car, too." As an afterthought, she added, "Just text me the details. No need to call back, okay?"

The temperature inside the Ford had cooled to about ninety. The little engine might have enough horsepower to run the cold air and move the vehicle at the same time. She pulled out of the parking lot, found her way onto I-30 west, and settled into a reasonable speed in the middle lane.

The speakerphone buzzed. She hit the button to answer without looking at the number. "Kimball."

"Morris here. You must be one of the luckiest reporters on

the planet. After weeks of nothing, I talk to you and an hour later, NOPD calls. Kowalski checked in."

"Can I talk to him?"

"Only if you know a good psychic. Checked in as a John Doe. The body is old. Decomposed. No ID. No missing person's report. They've had him on ice for a few days."

She exhaled. "Damn."

"I'll get details."

"Cyanide?"

"Unlikely."

"Why?"

"Because of the bullet hole in his head. There's an autopsy scheduled. I'll get the full report. You'll know right after me."

"That's everyone on the list."

"Except Grantly."

"You said he was clean."

"When you have eliminated the impossible, then whatever remains, *however improbable*, must be the truth."

"Occam?"

"Sherlock Holmes, actually."

She choked on the laugh. "But, you checked him out."

"Two months ago. When all this started."

Jess's eyes went wide. "Two months ago? Anything could have happened."

"I did tell you about the other eight cases begging for my attention, didn't I?"

"I thought it was seven?"

"That was before lunch."

She sighed. "I just booked a flight to New Orleans."

"Grantly's in Florida."

She poked her tongue out at the phone. "I'll get to Florida sometime later tonight or early tomorrow."

"That would be good. Check up on Grantly. It's been a few weeks since we talked to him, too."

"What am I? Your shoe leather? I've got a day job, you know."

"I thought you wanted to be on the team. I told you, I can't do everything. If you don't want to follow up with Grantly, it won't happen." He paused. "Can you live with that?"

She ran her fingers through her hair. A long stream of air escaped through straight lips. "This has to be a two-way street, Morris."

"I called you the minute I heard something, so don't give me that. Find me even a sliver of evidence, and I'll buy you a new pair of shoes."

She sighed. He'd known she'd agree before he placed the call. "I'll ring you from Orlando. Or from New Orleans, if I get anything useful there."

"Thanks, Jess. We owe you."

She punched the off button. "Bet your ass. And don't think I won't collect, Mr. FBI."

# CHAPTER NINE

JESS STOPPED IN THE Starbucks at some nameless junction on I-30 to check Mandy's text with her trip details. Flights were full. The next available seat was three hours away. She texted approval and asked Mandy to book a late flight to Orlando after New Orleans and change the hotel, too.

She ordered one of the fruit flavored iced teas, pulled out her laptop, and skimmed the highlights on Morris's flash drive.

She knew many of the details, but some she did not. Like Zmich, Warga and Supko barely had enough money for a Big Mac when they died. No wonder Candace Supko was living hand-to-mouth in that trailer park. *What about the other families? Wives, kids? Where were they now?* She'd find out something when she found Kowalski's contacts. Maybe something useful.

The autopsy reports for Zmich, Warga, and Supko were short and succinct. Cyanide poisoning was apparently easy to detect, assuming you knew how to read gas chromatograph charts. She didn't, but she trusted the medical examiners did.

She flipped over to the doctor's transcribed notes and compared the three cases. Without the Blazek connection, they would just be three sad stories. Three people who had been so overwhelmed that they had taken their own lives.

With only these seemingly narrow facts available, she could see how authorities in three separate locations, not communicating with each other, had believed each was a suicide. As Morris said, there was no evidence of foul play on the surface.

Depression wasn't always easy to spot. Not everyone wore their heart on their sleeves. And the available evidence seemed to point in only one direction.

She thought a minute about what these five might have in common besides their criminal enterprise. They were schoolmates. Middle-aged adult males. Americans. What else?

Blazek was all about announcing his situation to anyone and everyone, as if his lies were true. These files, thin as they were, suggested his pals had been tight-lipped about their financial situations. Every one of the survivors who were interviewed said the same thing. They hadn't known how despondent the dead man had been before he killed himself.

A cold chill ran down her arms despite the frigidly air-conditioned shop. She felt like a cartoon light bulb had flashed above her head.

She grabbed her drink and her laptop and bundled into her car. She dialed Morris and tapped her palm impatiently on the steering wheel until he picked up. "I need to see Blazek again."

"Why?"

"We missed something before."

"Like what?"

"I want to see him. Check something out."

"I'll have to request a meeting with him." He paused as if checking the time. "I'm not sure we can arrange it today before your flight."

Jess felt sure her hunch would pay off. But she didn't want to miss her flight to prove it. Wait around Dallas until tomorrow? No. Not in the cards. "How did you catch Blazek?"

"He deposited fifteen grand cash in his bank account. They report transactions that big. That came to our attention. We questioned him, and he just unraveled."

She smiled, wiped a palm over her face, and nodded. She had him. She could feel it. "Unraveled, huh? How *convenient*."

"What's that mean?"

"Oh, come on. A guy like Blazek makes a rookie mistake like that? He might as well have waved a red flag in front of the bulls of Pamplona."

"Jess—"

"Just have him ready, Henry. I'm not leaving without seeing him again in person. And I'm running short on time."

She heard his sigh as plainly as if he was sitting in the passenger seat of the little Ford, but she didn't care. She hung up and left the parking lot in a squeal of rubber.

# CHAPTER TEN

NOT LONG AGO, JESS had sat in the private visitor room waiting for Blazek the first time and the guard had told her Blazek wasn't happy about meeting with her again. She wasn't keen on seeing Blazek again either, but she was damn well going to. He'd played them all and she wouldn't let him get away with it.

As he'd done this morning, the deputy checked the room, and another deputy walked Blazek in. His head was down. He sat in the seat. The deputy gave him the same run down of rules, pointed to the camera, and turned to leave.

Jess held her hand up. "Wait."

The deputy looked at her.

She smiled. "I'd feel better if you stayed."

He looked at Blazek and her, and shrugged. He stood with his back to the corner, feet braced, hands folded. "Fifteen minutes."

"I won't take that long."

Blazek looked at the table. Whatever had fueled his bravado this morning had been extinguished in the short time since she'd seen him last. His sentence was too light, Jess felt. But now she wondered whether he'd survive long enough to serve it. He seemed to have given up already.

She frowned at him. "You knew, didn't you?"

He looked up at her and frowned.

"You knew they'd be killed."

He shrugged. "Who are you talking about?"

"You knew the operation was going south, so you got yourself arrested."

He wagged his head back and forth, but there was no energy in the movement. "I have no idea what you're talking about."

She slammed her palm on the table. "Don't give me that crap!"

The deputy shifted his weight.

"You're an investor in anything you can get your hands on." She stood and leaned forward as close as she could get without actually touching Blazek. "You know you can't simply walk bundles of cash into a bank without garnering a whole lot of attention. You knew a deposit that size would be reported. You knew it would be flagged and you'd be found out. You did it on purpose, didn't you?"

Blazek shrugged. "I made a mistake." His voice was calm. Flat.

"The only mistake you've made was thinking you could get away with your life. And you didn't care that your pals were about to lose theirs." She sneered. "What a guy."

He shook his head, but his enthusiasm wasn't there. He didn't bother to defend himself.

"You told me one true thing, though. You aren't the leader

of this pack of thieves." She narrowed her gaze and peered into his miserable soul. "But you *do* know who's running the team, don't you?"

"No." His lies came as easily as ever.

"And you knew what they were going to do. So you gathered whatever money you could salvage, and stashed it somewhere safe until you get out of prison."

"You're guessing."

She gestured to the room. "It's not nice living in here. You may not survive prison." She jerked her thumb toward the outside wall. "But you figured you were better off here than out there where you know for sure they can get to you. They can kill you easily. Just like Warga, Supko, and the others."

He continued to look straight ahead, vacantly, as if he didn't see her.

"You knew they would be murdered."

He threw his hands up. "I gave Agent Morris the same list of names as I gave you."

"And when he told you Kowalski had gone missing, you said nothing."

"How was I supposed to know he was dead? I was in jail!"

One guess confirmed. She didn't blink to show she'd noticed that Blazek had known Kowalski was dead when the FBI did not. "But you knew what was going to happen to Supko, didn't you?"

"I don't have to listen to this." He stood and the chair clanged to the floor, just as it had this morning. Drama. That's all. He took two steps toward the exit and the deputy moved forward.

Jess pushed herself between Blazek and the door, no table between them now. She tilted her head up to meet his gaze dead on. "They're dead. Four of your friends. Maybe the only friends you actually had. Horrible deaths. These men had families, Blazek. Kids. Wives. Parents. And you don't even care, do you?"

"I told Morris I was worried about them, didn't I? Told you, too."

"You're all heart."

"You think you can judge me? Get the hell out of my way." He stepped around her and moved toward the exit.

She clenched her fists. She wanted to pummel him, reduce him to a puddle on the floor. The guard took him by the arm, and steered him through the door. Blazek was an evil, lying, cunning bastard who—

He put his head around the door to taunt her one last time. "I'll tell you what though, girl genius. Grantly's still alive. Tells you something, doesn't it?"

The heavy steel door thumped closed.

Jess sank into her seat, still fuming. Blazek was a manipulative liar who should have been put away for life. Or death. Either way was fine with her at the moment.

But he had a point. Grantly? Alive? The odd one out?

She pulled the list from her pocket, and ran her finger down the names. Kowalski, Warga, Zmich, Supko, and Grantly.

Grantly. Last on the list. Number five out of five, and the only one alive.

Either he was the one who murdered his friends, or somewhere there was a cyanide pill with his name on it.

# CHAPTER ELEVEN

*New Orleans, Louisiana*
*May 10*

LATE TAKEOFF FROM DALLAS, as always, but the pilot made up time in the air and set the 737 down on the tarmac at Louis Armstrong Airport in New Orleans less than ninety minutes after takeoff. The short up and down flight was a blessing because she could make the quick stop before heading on to Grantly, and a curse because Jess only had time to review one of Morris's files, the one on Kowalski, which was briefer than a child's birthday wish list.

The FAA did not ban personal electronic devices in flight and the airlines were allowed to set their own rules. But most required devices to be turned off and stowed during takeoff and landing. On a short hop, the up and down took most of the flight time. She'd have to read the other files on the New Orleans-to-Orlando leg.

Morris had sent an email with the details about Kowalski's body that he'd received so far from New Orleans police. He'd included the names and addresses of Kowalski's next of kin, who had not yet been informed that Kowalski's body had been found. Morris's email said he might get more information and if he did, he'd send it on.

Kowalski's partially decomposed body had been found inside an ornate cemetery tomb with a crypt when the crypt was being prepared for one of its rightful owners. Morris had attached a photo of the historic above-ground vault at Forrest Lawn near the French Quarter. The tomb looked like an ornate house complete with an iron fence. Forrest Lawn was filled with similar tombs and looked like an eerie small city for the dead.

Whoever stashed Kowalski's body there must have believed the crypt would be undisturbed for quite a while. After a few months, Kowalski would have been indistinguishable from the others stored inside.

Morris had attached three photos of Kowalski's corpse. The positive identification had been made by dental records, Morris's note said. Two months was a long time to leave a body in a bag inside a damp crypt. Even aside from the damage done by the bullet.

Jess enlarged the photo enough to see what looked like an entrance wound made by a .22-caliber bullet through the soft tissues between his eyes. The gunshot might not have been the cause of death, though. She'd wait for the autopsy report for the final answer to that question.

She punched the cemetery's address into her phone's GPS. She'd need some photos for her article. She asked the limo driver, who had picked her up at the airport, to take a quick detour to Forrest Lawn.

"Nice place. You got people buried there?"

"Yes," she said, deliberately misconstruing his meaning.

Along the way, they passed the newer Metairie cemeteries and closer to the French Quarter, St. Louis Nos. 1, 2, and 3. The rows of tombs resembled residential streets. No wonder these places were called cities of the dead.

At Forrest Lawn, she gave the driver directions to the crypt where Kowalski's body was discovered. It was easy to locate. Yellow crime scene tape surrounded the small square building and a police officer was standing out front.

"Pull over for a minute, okay?"

The crypt was the same size and shape as a roomy garden shed. Granite. Maybe twenty feet square and ten feet high. The façade was engraved with the words "Family Tomb" and below that, "Zimmer." The door appeared to be granite as well. It had heavy brass hinges on one side. A five-foot, ornate iron fence complete with a double entry gate wide enough to accommodate a coffin and pall bearers surrounded the building.

The name niggled the deep recesses of her reptilian brain. Zimmer. She'd seen it before. Recently. She reached for the data from her subconscious and remembered where she'd seen it. Zimmer was the artist's signature on Candace Supko's last painting.

"Did you want to get out here, ma'am?" her driver asked.

"Yes. I do. For a few minutes. Thanks." Jess slipped out of the limo and shot a few photos to go with her *Taboo* piece from across the road and slipped the phone back into her pocket.

The police officer on duty was young. Mid-twenties, maybe. Tall, dark, and handsome. He watched her approach without comment. If he'd seen her shooting pictures, he didn't object. The silver nameplate on his chest said "R. Galet."

"I'm Jessica Kimball. I'm working with FBI Special Agent Henry Morris." She extended her hand first and he shook it. A good start. She had her business card ready if he asked for it.

"Morris called my boss a couple of hours ago and said you'd be coming by. I'm supposed to answer your questions, show you whatever you want to see, and then get back to my beat."

"I understand you found a body inside this crypt yesterday that didn't belong here. Is that right?"

Galet nodded toward the crypt. "Happens all the time. Nothing illegal about putting multiple bodies in a family vault."

Jess arched her eyebrows. "I didn't know that."

"By law, every two years the families can place a previously buried loved one into a special body bag, destroy the coffin, and add another member to the vault." He shrugged. "We can't bury most people underground here because the water table is too high and we don't have enough above-ground burial space in all of New Orleans. We've had to make adjustments."

The information creeped Jess out, though. She shivered in the bright sunshine. "So what made this particular body suspicious, then?"

"A teenager died unexpectedly over the weekend in a car wreck. When they were preparing for the funeral, the unidentified body was found inside the vault. No coffin. No body bag. The family who owns this crypt hadn't buried anyone here for about ten years and no one in the family recognized him. Although the guy had been in there a while and wasn't, well let's say pleasant to look at."

"Were you the first officer on the scene here when they found the body?"

"No. Never been here before. Never saw the body." He shook his head and shrugged again. "Came on about thirty minutes ago."

"Can I look inside? Take a few photos?"

"Like I said, my orders are to show you whatever you want to see. If you can look at it, you can photograph it, I guess. I'd ask you to be respectful of the family, though. They've just lost a boy and they can't bury him properly until this mess is cleared up. The family is pretty upset."

"Of course. I understand."

Galet stepped aside and opened the heavy door to the crypt. Jess snapped a few photos before she looked inside. There were no lights or illumination of any kind. She turned her phone on for the soft blue backlight and used it to look around. The square room was plain, cool, and dry. Not remarkable in any way except that it held coffins stacked on either side.

"Where was the body found?"

"On the floor. Dead center." But for the circumstances, Jess would have groaned at his exceedingly bad pun.

The floor of the crypt was also granite. She held her phone to illuminate the center of the floor, but didn't see anything indicating a body had been decomposing there yesterday.

"Any trace evidence found in here?"

Galet shrugged. "This isn't even my case."

Jess stepped back out into the sunlight, which felt warm and inviting all of a sudden. Galet closed the heavy door and they walked through the iron gates and away from the crypt.

"If I think of anything else, can I call you?" Jess reached out to shake hands again. This time, she gave him her card.

"I don't know what more I can possibly tell you, but sure." He reached into his pocket and handed over one of his. "You'd be better off talking to the detective assigned to the case. Or ask Morris. I'm sure he can find out, if he doesn't know already."

"What about the Zimmer family?"

Galet cocked his head and peered as if he didn't understand. "I mean, it's likely the dead man was connected to them in some way. Otherwise, how would anyone have managed to get a body inside there?"

Galet shrugged.

*Indeed.* Another question for Morris. Jess added it to her mental list.

# CHAPTER TWELVE

KOWALSKI HAD LIVED IN a rented condo located in the historic Garden District of New Orleans. Jess gave her driver Kowalski's address. The wide lawns and lush gardens of what had once been plantations were both breathtaking and a little creepy.

The limo pulled to a stop in front of 1877 Coliseum. Set back from the street on a deep green lawn was a Greek Italianate building that had been converted from a single home to eight apartments and then to four condos, according to the quick web search Jess did on her phone. Kowalski's condo was the one on the top right.

Tall bushes on the inside and an ornate iron fence on the street side lined the lot and kept the riff-raff out. Jess walked along the sidewalk to the front gate, which was not locked. The hinges of the heavy iron gate squealed when she pushed it wide enough to slip through and again when she closed it.

Ten yards along a straight paved path from the sidewalk,

Jess ran up the steps to the front door. On one side of the heavy wood entrance was a row of four engraved brass plates, each with its own button.

Number three sported Kowalski's name, which made sense if the home had been divided into equal quarters. Jess pressed the button twice and waited. After a few moments of nothing happening, she pressed the button twice more. Same result.

Okay. Maybe Kowalski had lived alone. Maybe his neighbors were working. Coming here was a long shot. She'd had good luck interviewing neighbors in the past, but Kowalski probably wasn't the type to confide in friends.

Morris had supplied an office address. She'd try that next. Employees and co-workers should have more information about him anyway.

She was halfway down the stairs when she heard the heavy door open behind her. She turned. A man wearing nothing but a towel stood half hidden in the shadows.

"Sorry. I was in the shower. I was expecting someone else." He was maybe thirty. Tall. Fit. He tousled long dark hair with the second towel in his left hand. "Can I help you?"

Jess tromped up the steps again. "I'm looking for Aleksy Kowalski."

"You found him."

So Kowalski had a son. That info wasn't in Morris's file. Jess extended her hand. "I'm Jessica Kimball. *Taboo Magazine.*"

"Seriously?" He raked his hands through his hair to tame it a bit.

His naked chest was well-muscled, tanned, and totally hairless. Probably a wax job, judging from all the curly hair on his arms and legs. Ouch. That's gotta hurt.

"Yep." Jess fished out one of her business cards and held it out. He retrieved the card and examined it for a moment. "No offense, but the Aleksy Kowalski I'm looking for is maybe late forties. Either you're remarkably youthful for your age, or I have the wrong man."

"You probably want my uncle. Dad's brother." He looked at Jess and flipped her business card across his fingers, which sounded like a playing card *thwapping* the spokes of a kid's bicycle. "Before you ask, I don't know where my uncle is. He lives here with me, but I haven't seen him in a few months, actually. He travels a lot on business."

"What kind of business is he in?"

"International banking and investments. Why? *Taboo* can't be interested in something boring like that?"

He seemed to be flexing his abs or something. He made no move to brush her off. "What about your Dad? Is he around?"

"Sorry. Dad lives in New York."

"Mrs. Kowalski, then?"

He grinned. "You mean my aunt, not my mom, right?"

At this point, Jess would have accepted either, but she nodded to avoid suspicion.

"Well, Aunt Katia passed away a few years ago. Breast cancer. And before you ask, they didn't have any kids."

"I see. And your mother?"

He cocked his head. His eyes narrowed. Maybe she'd gone a bridge too far with that question. Men usually protected their mothers forever, in Jess's experience. His tone was a little frosty. "In New York. Where she lives. Anything else?"

Jess flailed around trying to think of something legitimate to prolong the conversation and maybe get a lead to follow. "Uh, anybody else been here looking for your uncle?"

"Like who?"

She shrugged. "Anyone at all."

"Why would anybody be looking for him?"

This was going nowhere and she was wasting time. "You're right. Well, you have my card. When he gets back, please ask your uncle to call me. Sorry to bother you."

She pivoted and made it halfway down the steps again before he said, "I won't be able to do that."

She looked up at him from the fourth step. "Why not?"

"Because he's not coming back. His job sent him to China. Probably be gone for a five-year stint, he said."

"*China?*"

"American companies are doing a lot of business over there these days." Aleksy smirked. His voice dripped condescension. "Or hadn't you heard?"

Jess nodded slowly. She'd been holding her phone behind her back. She pressed the button to turn it on and used the thumbprint recognition to gain access to the camera. "How about you and your dad, Mr. Kowalski? Do you three have a family business going here?"

Before he answered, in one smooth motion, she pulled the phone around, lifted it, and snapped a few photo bursts of the very much alive Aleksy Kowalski. Photos were always better than physical descriptions, should he turn out to be something other than what he claimed.

"I can't imagine how my business can possibly concern you," he said before he stepped back into the shadows and closed the heavy door with a sturdy thud.

# CHAPTER THIRTEEN

*Orlando, Florida*
*May 10*

THE FLIGHT ACROSS THE Gulf of Mexico from New Orleans was easy. By the time the 737 landed smoothly in Orlando, Jess was only halfway through Morris's files. She'd go over every bit and byte of these files tonight. For sure.

The reports showed Warga, Zmich, and Supko had died within a few days of each other, two months earlier. Kowalski's body was decomposed at a level suggesting he'd died at the same time.

The very same time Blazek was, in his own special way, getting himself into police protection. He knew what was going down, and there was blood on his hands just as surely as if he'd poisoned the other members of the gang himself.

She furrowed her brow and tapped her fingernail against her eye tooth. If someone was cleaning house, Grantly was either not on the list, or he was the one doing the cleaning.

And if the murderer wasn't Grantly, they had a good reason

for keeping him alive. Perhaps his rank in whatever sick organization they belonged to?

She pulled out the address Morris had given her. It was clearly a business address, Grantly's real estate firm.

She stuffed the address back into her bag, along with her laptop, and waited in line to exit the plane. Once off the jet bridge, she called Morris.

"Morris here."

"Warga, Zmich, and Supko were broke when they were killed, right?" She walked around a woman with a baby in a stroller. No moving sidewalks anywhere in sight.

"Pretty much penniless. There might have been some life insurance."

"Kowalski was likely broke, too. You're looking into that?"

"Yeah. Although that condo the nephew is living in has a market value in the seven-figure range, according to tax records."

She shifted the heavy laptop case to her left shoulder, waiting for the tram to take her to the main terminal. "That's why Grantly's still alive. He's got money left, and they're going to extract it from him first."

Morris paused. "Could be."

"It has to be. That's what these people want. Money."

"Maybe. Easier to hold a gun to their heads to get the money, though."

Jess clicked her tongue against the roof of her mouth. "Because before they were running a team of scammers. Each one generating revenue from the people they brought into the operation. Now they're squeezing the last they can from the whole tree."

The tram pulled into the station and the doors slid open on

both sides. Passengers exited on the north side and Jess entered on the opposite.

"Sorry. What?" She pressed her palm over her ear to hear Morris's voice over the loudspeakers telling passengers to hold onto the handrails firmly in two languages.

"Because they're closing it down."

"Yeah. Closing up shop. Disposing of the…" she glanced around at the passengers jammed into the tram and pressing against her on all sides, "…problems."

"I don't think so." Morris paused. "They're just moving on. Starting on a new batch of victims. Sucking more people into their web."

"I have to talk to Grantly. Work my way into his confidence. He has to have been lying when he talked to you. We have to find something."

Morris laughed. "Good plan."

"Yeah, well. Shoe leather. No way around it, is there?"

"I'm flexible. Just find me something I can take to a judge and we're back in business."

"Keep that judge on speed dial. And meanwhile, can you check out the last name Zimmer?"

"I guess I can. Why?"

"Candace Supko told me her husband invested in bad art. She said he always managed to sell the paintings at a profit to private collectors."

"Yeah? So what?"

"Well, she said the art was bad, as in worthless. And she had one painting on the wall of her mobile home. It was signed by Zimmer. The same name that's on the tomb where they found Kowalski's body."

"I see. I'll check it out." She could hear the keys clicking on a keyboard. Morris was taking notes. "Anything else?"

"Not yet. I'll call you later."

She hung up, and felt the weight of her foolish boast as she followed the crowds to baggage claim. The bags were already on the carousel by the time she got there. She preferred to travel with only a carry-on but her concealed carry permit didn't allow the Glock in the cabin.

An hour later, she'd collected her luggage and found her rental, a small foreign SUV. She stowed her bags in the very back, and placed her Glock under the front seat where she could easily reach it.

It was dark in Orlando. She hated to conduct recon while driving at night in unfamiliar surroundings. It was inefficient, for one thing, too easy to miss the important things, and it was too easy to end up in the wrong part of town.

She entered Grantly's Winter Park address into the GPS on her phone, adjusted the mirrors and steering wheel, and cruised out of the garage.

Her destination was fourteen miles northwest of the Orlando airport. She could be there in less than thirty minutes. Mandy had booked a chain hotel nearby and texted the confirmation. So far, so good. She'd had a long and exhausting day. A hot bath and a comfortable bed sounded like a heavenly combination.

She drove through several residential areas that ran the gamut from stately historic homes to recently constructed condominium towers. She had no home address for Grantly, which was fine. Grantly could wait until tomorrow. She needed to be on the top of her game for the interview, not on the backend of a long day dealing with scum like Blazek.

She arrived in Winter Park, and turned onto the main street, Park Avenue. The office of Grantly & Son was on the left hand side. She slowed to a crawl. Under the streetlights, the paint had an odd but rich glow.

Pictures and property details jostled for position in the plate glass window. Behind the photos inside the building looked to be desks. Not the cubicles of a modern office, but large wood objects with carved legs, banker's lamps, and blotters. The opening hours were painted on the door: Grantly & Son would be open for business at 7:00 a.m.

She eased on down the street. The shops along Park Avenue were closed for the night, but the old storefronts looked prosperous. Farther down Central, the park that gave the area its name was deserted, although the fountain splashed water as if enthralled admirers were watching.

If Peter hadn't been taken, it was the sort of place she would have liked to live. Somewhere that had charm. A little uniqueness, a little independent spirit. Local shops and local people. Not deep in the city, but not far out in the faceless suburbs. She sighed. One day she would find him. One day she would call a place like Winter Park, home. They both would. Her eyes swam with glassy tears but she blinked them back and turned toward her hotel. Crying over Peter wouldn't help. She knew that much for sure.

By the time she checked in, and took a quick shower, she was too exhausted to think.

Tomorrow she would be ready for Grantly. She would be bright, and primped, and full of smiles. She would laugh at every joke he cracked. She would smile knowingly at every shared experience. She would bring the lure of fame to his doorstep…and she would nail the bastard.

Whatever his involvement. Whatever his part in the grand scheme. Whatever he thought he was going to get away with.

She would find something. Something to stop him, stop the others, stop Blazek. Especially Blazek.

When she was done, she would take a couple of days off. She needed it. She would shove all and everything to the back of her mind, and she would eat, drink, and sleep like an angel. She sighed, especially at the sleep part.

Jess was no stranger to sleep deprivation. When she was this tired, memories of the night her son was kidnapped felt strong and fresh. As she sat on the edge of her bed, and dialed her tip lines to check for news of Peter, unwelcome emotions from ten years ago flooded over her.

The crappy apartment. Pregnant at sixteen, trying to get through high school and on to college. She'd wanted a good life for Peter and she'd known she needed an education to make everything she wanted for him to become reality.

She closed her eyes, hung her head, and let the feelings flood back. She'd been exhausted that night, too. Working as a waitress at a low-rent diner. Peter was a colicky baby. He cried all the time and rarely slept. Her exhaustion then was total, despair of the spirit, really.

When Peter had finally managed to nap that long ago night, she'd dashed to grab the laundry from the basement.

She'd only left him for the briefest of moments. When she ran back to the apartment, he was gone.

Peter had never been found, although finding him remained Jess's personal obsession to this day. At first, she'd believed the authorities who told her they'd find Peter. She'd left the job to the experts. Until she'd finished school and finally realized that they'd given up.

Oh, they claimed they were still working on Peter's case. But the resources weren't there. They had moved on. She didn't blame them, really. But she couldn't do the same.

She took this job with *Taboo*, an international magazine, so she could travel wherever she needed to go and get the national exposure that might allow Peter to find her. Or anyone with information about him to know how to reach her.

She'd followed every lead, no matter how unlikely. Every extra penny she earned went into her search. Age-progression software created pictures of Peter as he might appear now. She carried those pictures with her and posted them everywhere. She'd used every ounce of her investigative skills to find him. With no success.

For now, seeking justice for victims like herself and the people Blazek cheated in a society more focused on protecting the killers kept her soul alive while she searched for Peter. Barely.

There was nothing on the tip lines, as usual. Nothing from the four investigators she'd hired in different regions of the country. But she would never stop. Never forget every moment of the night he was taken, ignore the horrors he might be going through, nor forgive her own failure. Never.

She lay down on the bed in the Orlando hotel room, dark thoughts swirling. Disturbing dreams controlled her sleep regardless of where she slept each night.

A few years before, a professor at Stanford University had taught her techniques to manage the nightmares. She had listened and learned the method. Meditate. Focus on the positive. Bright and shiny thoughts. Simple pleasures. Fresh cotton, green fields, the crunch of newly fallen snow. Happy memories. Family celebrations. A shared past. A future to long for. Drift into peace.

She remembered everything he had said, but she was too exhausted to heed his advice.

She slipped into sleep where her familiar demons lurked.

# CHAPTER FOURTEEN

*Denver, 3:37 AM*
*6 years earlier*

NIGHT SHIFTS WERE LIKE this. She's edgy and dulled at the same time. Exhausted, hungry, her stomach growls. It's late. She wants to leave, but she has more of the endless work to complete before she can rest. She notices everything. Takes notes. Later, she'll write a compelling story. Again.

She is seated opposite the desk in the prosecutor's office, a war zone of its own kind. The room is small and cheaply furnished. The desk has been abused by dozens of young prosecutors. Her pantyhose are snagged where a gouge in the wood caught her left thigh earlier, leaving an angry red scratch on lightly-tanned skin. She feels the still-fresh stinging. She is cold in the drafty room. Her nipples are visible through her bra and the pink silk blouse she's wearing. The rose scent from the candle burning on the window sill tickles her nostrils but can't hide the stench of fear in the room because that stink has seeped into the walls and carpet like old cigar smoke.

Glaring fluorescent lights overhead cast a green hue on Jess's blonde hair. Mr. and Mrs. Axel are seated in the plastic chairs, waiting for the prosecutor to review their petition, to sign the request for a restraining order against the worthless slime who has been threatening their five-year-old daughter. The form is incomplete, only a few of the blank lines filled out in shaky blue ballpoint, skips in the ink where Mr. Axel has tried to write over the greasy spots on the page. The prosecutor smooths the folds from the paper, feels its rough edges.

Mr. Axel is about the prosecutor's age, Jess thinks. Mrs. Axel appears a bit younger. Unlike most of the unending train of victims Jess has interviewed during her final college internship, Mr. Axel is neatly dressed. He's wearing polished shoes and black socks instead of scuffed sneakers and white ones.

His khakis are inexpertly pressed, the fresh crease is sharper than the ghosts of its predecessors. His blue striped cotton shirt is pressed, too, but the collar isn't stiffened by starch nor the placket crisply flat. A logo over the breast pocket declares he works for Grand Gardens, a local tourist attraction. The prosecutor doesn't know or care what work Mr. Axel performs there, so Jess makes a note to find out.

Mrs. Axel's sweaty hands lay one over the other on the black vinyl shoulder bag in her lap. When she moves slightly, damp palm prints remain. Mrs. Axel has said nothing since she arrived.

Her husband does all the talking.

"He drives by our house. When little Tia is outside, he blows the horn and scares her. He turns up the music in his car to make the ground shake. My wife—he drives right up behind her and slams on his brakes. They squeal so loud she thinks he's going to hit her with his car." Mr. Axel's heavy accent is hard to place. Is it Russian? Polish? Slavic of some kind, Jess thinks, from his Caucasian features. Again unlike many of the crime victims she's followed who have been mostly Latino so far.

Mrs. Axel shudders, lowers her head and covers her eyes briefly with her left hand. Jess notices tears on Mrs. Axel's cheeks. The woman is afraid, terrified for herself and her family.

"Why is he angry with you?" the prosecutor asks.

"We've done nothing, I swear! He says we've complained about him to the police. He says we turned him in for selling drugs. But we didn't! We didn't!" Mr. Axel's agitated pleading causes his wife to cry softly.

The prosecutor sits, unmoved, too burned out to attend to the depth of their fear. He has heard so many stories that were much worse. Children murdered, tortured, molested. Women beaten, raped, cut with knives. Men gunned down in front of their homes, or at their jobs. Only two years into the job, and already he'd lost his empathy.

But Jess still felt it.

The prosecutor takes the badly printed application, crumples it up, and drops it in the trash. He pulls a fresh form from his desk and reviews the questions, slowly, carefully, completely. This time, when he asks whether the angry neighbor has been violent or threatened violence, Mr. Axel says, "Yes. He threw eggs at our house. He ran over our lawn with his car."

Mrs. Axel speaks for the first time. Softly, with grace. "He pushed me today on the sidewalk. I fell down." She demurely raises her skirt a few inches to display a viciously battered knee, still bloody and too fresh for scabs.

Jess sees the prosecutor write with a felt-tip marker while he recites, "stalking behavior, assault, battery," on the correct line of the form.

*He puts the cap on the marker and slides it into his shirt pocket, tells the Axels, "You wait here. I'll take this downstairs, get the night judge to sign it, and I'll send a uniformed police officer home with you to watch your house tonight."*

*He raises himself up from the squeaking chair, slips stiff loafers onto swollen feet, slides his arms into a wrinkled gray jacket and hurries down the corridor.*

*When he returns to the dingy office, Tia is in the room, too. She's a perfect little girl. Dark hair, like her mommy. Liquid brown eyes, flawless olive skin, already missing a front tooth.*

*"How old are you?" Jess asks her, although she knows the answer.*

*Tia holds up her hand, all five fingers splayed. She says, "I'll be in kindergarten this year. My mommy's going, too. She's a teacher's aide. My daddy's coach of our soccer team."*

*"You bet we are," Mr. Axel says, as he lifts his daughter in his arms. Mrs. Axel smiles with hope. They believe the harried prosecutor. Rely on him. Trust his promises.*

*Jess had done that once. In the past. Maybe this prosecutor would be different. Maybe the Axels wouldn't be sorry.*

*The prosecutor walks them down the hallway, and introduces them to the uniformed police officer who will take them home, and watch over them until Tia goes to college. Or until the low-life drug dealer shoots up an overdose, and kills himself. Or one of the other gang bangers in the neighborhood takes him out.*

*It could have happened like that. It should have happened like that.*

*But it didn't.*

*Later that night, the sky is clear, cold. The full moon is nature's only night-light. Thin frost shimmers on the grass. Jess is standing in front of the scum's house. The Axels are outside across the street. Mr. Axel is watering the lawn while Mrs. Axel trims dead blooms from red roses. Tia rides a scooter standing up, back and forth along the sidewalk. She calls out, "Hi, Jess!" Jess waves to her. She laughs. Her parents wave back.*

*Jess removes her gun from its holster. She walks up the long sidewalk to the killer's front door, and rings the bell. When he opens the door, she lifts her right arm straight out, holding the Glock as she'd been trained to do.*

*She squeezes the trigger repeatedly and puts three rounds right into his laughing face. His head blows apart and splatters all over the wall, the door, her.*

*His warm blood is on her face. But she doesn't stop. She shoots again and again. The gun booming, the walls shaking, the man screaming. She empties the clip into his body, and the smell of gunfire tingles in her nose.*

SHE JERKED UPRIGHT IN the bed, her clenched fists in front of her. She looked around, not recognizing her surroundings. She pushed the covers aside, and stumbled from her bed.

Nothing had changed. The scum was dead, but Jess didn't kill him. Tia started kindergarten. But her mommy was no longer a teacher's aide, and her daddy no longer coached soccer.

Jess stumbled to the bathroom, flipped on the light, and splashed cool water over her face and neck. She looked at the clear water draining from the basin.

She didn't have the killer's blood on her face. It had never been on her face. It was on her hands. Always on her hands. No matter how she tried, it would not fade nor wash off. It was as real as the ground under her feet. Even if no one could see it but her.

When the man who'd threatened the Axels murdered them in their front yard, he'd shot himself. There and then. In the same front yard. Beside the tree Tia had learned to climb. On the spot where her father had played ball with her. Where her mother had shared her picnics with a stuffed bear, and each and every one of her dollies.

The neighbors had bolted their doors. Drawn their curtains. Hunkered down. They knew at the first shot what had happened. They needed no news crew, or police investigation. The dark clouds they had watched gathering on the horizon finally turning to a storm of gunpowder and hot metal.

Tia had called the police. The first number she had ever really remembered. The one her mother and father had taught her while they prayed she would never have cause to use it. Nine one one. One digit for each of the bodies lying in her garden.

The prosecutor had resigned the next day.

He had vowed never to turn another deserving client away, never to let the gap between what the law promised and what it could deliver take another innocent life.

It was a promise he meant to keep. He said it every day for six months. At breakfast, at lunch, and into many, many late nights.

Every day.

Every day until gang members drove by. Tattoos on their faces. Chemicals in their blood stream. Guns blazing.

She'd never trusted the justice system again. The Axel family was the system's second strike. No reason to give up a third.

Jess sighed. She straightened her back, and dried her face. She slipped on the hotel robe, snugging the belt around her waist. She blew out a long breath. Sleep was impossible. Work was the answer.

As it had been every day since Peter was taken.

She sat on the side of the bed, and dialed room service. It took less than five minutes for piping hot coffee to arrive at her door.

She poured a generous portion into a bowl-sized cup, and smelled the rich aroma. It was good coffee. Dark but not burnt. Strong but not thick. She gulped and swallowed.

The past would always haunt her. She could do nothing about what had gone before. She could only hope to do better next time.

Tomorrow, if all went well, the job would be over. She would know what Grantly was hiding. With luck, she would find the link Morris needed. She would have the evidence. He could enforce the law. And hopefully some form of justice would be offered to the victims.

She wanted justice. She craved it. She needed it.

For the people Blazek had scammed, the ones they knew about, the ones they had yet to find.

For Peter.

She had promised him that. She had promised herself that. She would find him. She felt it, every moment of every day. She wouldn't give up. Not until they were together again. A family.

Until then she would help every other victim she found. With her head and her hands and her heart, and if need be, her shoe leather. Whatever they needed. Whatever she could do. She couldn't ignore them. She wouldn't ignore them.

She didn't want to.

And Morris had asked her to help.

So she would.

Hell, yes.

# CHAPTER FIFTEEN

*Oganee, Florida*
*May 11*

LUIGI FICARRA AWOKE TO the sound of a motel alarm clock. An unpretentious shrill buzz. His body had barely entered into deep sleep an hour before. He slapped the clock off the table and across the room. Its electrical cord jerked out of the wall. The alarm went silent. His eyelids drifted closed. He felt himself drift down into sleep.

The alarm clock buzzed again.

He shook his head, and pried his eyes open. He squinted at the black plastic clock on the floor. It must have been equipped with a backup battery because the red display seemed to light the whole room. 3:00 a.m. He breathed deeply. No one in his right mind wanted to wake up at three in the morning.

He stretched his arms above his head, inhaling and exhaling. He rotated his head around, stretching his neck. He ran his palm over his face and felt the abrasion from the dark, heavy whiskers on his chin. No matter what the time, he had a job to do.

He shoved back the paper-thin bedclothes, and swung his legs over the edge of the bed and tousled black, curly hair with both hands. He stretched his arms above his head and groaned. His muscles felt tight.

He caught a glimpse of himself in the cheap mirror across the room. His build was lean and medium, but he wasn't in great shape at the moment. Too much surveillance time spent sitting on his ass.

If he'd been home, he would have made himself an espresso. Not here. This was the cheapest no-tell motel in the area. Hot coffee was unlikely and espresso impossible.

The room smelled musty and damp. The air-conditioner under the front window roared and rattled, but did little to remove humidity or lower the temperature. He wiped sweat from his brow.

He hadn't chosen the Oganee Motel for its creature comforts and elegance. Indeed, he'd driven away from the thriving hotels in the Orlando area and off the main highways to find a dump like this.

The motel was located outside the tiny country town of Oganee. When central Florida was a prosperous ranching community fifty years ago, the motel might have been the best place for guests to bunk. Now, the entire town was long past its prime and the motel was as decrepit as the rest of the place.

A potholed parking lot abutted the long, low block of rooms. Once, parking spaces had been marked with straight white lines, one space immediately in front of the door to each room. The paint had faded and worn, too.

It was the kind of place that rented by the hour. Couples who didn't want to be recognized or traced. Cheating husbands and unfaithful wives. Fifty-year-old bankers from the city who couldn't afford the scandal. Maybe a few engaged in sordid sex games. Others were excited enough by the forbidden thrills of illicit behavior.

Luigi shrugged. People were the same, the world over. He knew such people avoided better lodging where wide-angle cameras behind the registration desks would be routine. The Oganee Motel clerks were unlikely to go spreading customer names and photos around nearby towns. Residents here craved anonymity and were prepared to forgo the luxuries of comfort and hygiene to get it. Such was the power of secret lust and fetish.

Luigi laughed to himself. He didn't suffer from unseen forces of moral dignity that directed so many lives. Weaker people. People who would sacrifice their self-respect for a moment's excitement.

Luigi knew what he wanted, and when he wanted it, he took it. Not groveling. Not in secret. Not laden with shame. He looked people who sought to judge him directly in the eye and bested them with little more than a cold glare.

The annoying alarm's buzz sounded again. Luigi yawned. He had plenty of time, but he was in no mood to waste any of it. He walked across the room and thumped the alarm's off button. The buzzer gave a last desperate squawk before going silent. The LED glowed 3:04 a.m.

He padded his way across the disgustingly sticky carpet to the bathroom. White tiles covered the floor and walls. Dark black mold stains inhabited the corners and had taken root in the grout between the tiles. He grimaced. The whole room was a vacation mecca for all the germs in Florida.

He turned on the shower. Despite the motel's decrepit condition and compromised morals, the water flowed hot and plentiful. He stripped off his t-shirt and briefs and stepped under the stream. He opened one eye and glanced around the shower. No shampoo.

He reached out and grabbed the postage-stamp-sized hand soap from the sink. He rubbed the soap between his palms and added a bit of water. It made a weak lather. He started with his hair and worked his way down his body.

The soap left his hair in spiky lumps. He ducked his head under the streaming hot water and smoothed his hair down. He scraped the whiskers off his face with a disposable razor inadequate for the job. He touched the shower knob with his foot to shut off the water and stepped out.

Two towels hung on a rail that might once have been chrome. The towels were thin and small swatches of threadbare terry. He swiped them both over his body, pushing the dampness over his skin without feeling much drier. He used one to blot his hair.

He looked into the mirror briefly and shook his head. "Your eyes are bloodshot." He widened his brown eyes and turned his head this way and that to assess the redness. He ran a finger over his fuzzy eyebrows to tame them. "You look like a terrorist. How are you going to get a woman looking like that?"

He laughed. Finding women to share his bed had never been a problem for Luigi. Women told him he was dark and dangerous. He shrugged and tossed the damp fabric into a plastic bag.

He twisted the temperature setting on the AC unit to its lowest, but it made no difference to the breeze wafting from the vent.

He shrugged on his clothes, fighting their desire to stick to his damp skin. He collected his belongings and stuffed them into his overnight bag. He took the razor and the soap from the bathroom and placed them into the plastic bag with the towels.

He pulled on a pair of latex gloves, opened a bag of disinfectant cloths pre-wetted with bleach, and wiped down the bedside table. He cleaned the alarm clock and the lamp and replaced the clock on the table. He ran a fresh bleach cloth over the headboard and the chest of drawers, paying special attention to the handles.

He cleaned the front door and the doorknob and then took on the bathroom, wiping the surfaces and the taps. He opened a small bottle of bleach and splashed it liberally in the sink, bathtub, and toilet.

He ran the water in the sink and the bathtub for a while, and flushed the toilet several times.

When he was finished the entire room smelled of bleach. His prints were gone and there was little chance of anyone tracing his DNA, should anyone have cause to bother. He shuddered to think what a DNA search would uncover here especially because the room contained so much residual DNA before he checked in.

He bundled the bleach wipes into the plastic bag, crushing them down on the razor and soap. He wiped the plastic room key card and added it to the bag. When he was miles away, he'd find a good disposal option. Nothing would be linked to him.

He used the last disinfectant cloth to open the front door and to close it firmly behind him.

The air outside was milky white. A thick mist swirled around the motel's neon sign. He couldn't see the far end of the motel less than thirty yards away. He cursed in Italian. He had twenty-five miles to drive. The poor visibility would slow him down.

His heartbeat quickened. He felt heat flush from his neck to his hairline. He flexed his fists and then took a couple of deep breaths to temper his anger. He'd built extra time into his plans. He'd make it.

He pulled off the gloves, unlocked his white compact rental car, and threw his overnight bag on the rear seat. He stuffed the plastic bag in the passenger foot-well, close enough that he could easily reach over and throw it out when the chance arose.

The little white compact started easily. He reversed and zipped around to pull out onto what constituted the main two-lane road. There were no buildings and no streetlights nearby. The motel was a couple of miles out of town, just as its customers wanted. He turned left, weaving until he found the far side of the road. The rental's lights barely illuminated ten feet in front of him. He cursed his lack of cat's eyes that could see in the fog and crawled along the road.

He passed a sign indicating the little town of Sydney was one mile ahead. He ran through his route in his head. U.S. back road routes were deceptive. Long straight roads invited relaxed driving. They lulled him into near somnolence, particularly when he'd had so little sleep. Yet one missed turn could lead him in the wrong direction and might not be discovered for miles.

The fog thinned out. Not much, but enough to see the trees on either side of the road. He picked up his speed. The faint glow of life appeared in front of him. Sydney, according to the town limit sign.

He passed a twenty-four hour greasy spoon, lights on but no cars in the parking lot. He entered the center of the empty town. Streetlights helped illuminate the road, at least. Small shops lined the sidewalks. A few had left lights on for security, but Luigi saw no one inside the buildings.

He slowed at the red light in the very center of the tiny town.

He sneered. This place was the definitive middle of nowhere. He looked at the rental's clock and back at the red light. What was he slowing for? Not a soul was anywhere around and he was running late thanks to the fog.

Luigi jammed his foot down on the accelerator. The rental's little engine groaned, the gearbox changed down, and the sound grew to a thrashing wail.

The car jerked forward, leaning back on its suspension as it picked up speed. Luigi raced through the light. He needed to hurry. He didn't know what lay ahead.

He passed a used car lot and a Starbucks loomed ahead. His mouth salivated. Caffeine. About a gallon of the stuff would be welcome right now. But as he approached, he saw the Starbucks wouldn't be open for hours. He sped past.

A light appeared in his rearview mirror. Two lights. Headlights. A car, all the way back at the intersection by the red blinking traffic light.

He slowed a fraction. The car turned onto the main road and traveled in Luigi's direction.

He checked his speed. Forty-five. The car behind was gaining on him.

The streetlights ran out at the end of the last block. A few ranch-style houses, dark still at this hour, dotted the sides of the road. In a moment, even they ran out.

Behind him the car was three lengths back. Red and blue lights flicked brightly in the morning darkness. Cops.

Luigi swore. There was nothing he hated more than the routine traffic stop. Not that a couple of cops worried him. He was fast enough, and armed well enough, to handle them. It was the whole law enforcement machine that would be put in motion afterward that worried him.

Traffic stops were called in before the officers approached the stopped vehicle. Dispatchers kept track. They waited to check names and addresses, run license plates or driver's license numbers.

When Luigi was stopped, none of those routines would happen. Dispatchers quickly found the officers non-responsive to radio calls.

Then the machine would kick in.

Alerts would be issued. GPS trackers would identify the cruiser's location. Dashboard cameras, and even body-mounted cameras, were expected to identify him.

Nothing drew police attention faster than "officer down."

Luigi didn't care about confrontation or killing a policeman. He had zero interest in allowing a traffic stop to end his successful run. He was worthy of much better.

The police cruiser gained on him. Luigi didn't slow. There was always the chance they had received a distress call and would race past him.

There were no houses on either side of the road now. Thick trees and vegetation. Nothing else. He had left the city limits of Sydney. Maybe in the strange way of U.S. police departments, the cruiser would be out of its jurisdiction. Which would solve a lot of issues.

The cruiser slowed, falling in behind him. It wasn't going to pass. It wasn't responding to a distress call. The cops were stopping him.

The cruiser's red and blue lights washed over his car making it more difficult to see through the heavy fog. He leaned forward and peered into the soup. He needed to see.

Luigi was a careful man. He needed a good place to pull over. Not on the main road. Not out in the open. He hadn't seen another vehicle for miles, but that didn't mean he wouldn't see one at the most inopportune moment.

The dense trees offered little hope of a side road, but he kept looking.

The cruiser triggered its siren. One *woop-woop*. Sufficient to make the point, but not enough to wake the neighborhood, assuming there were homes nearby.

Luigi looked left and right. He saw no neighborhood.

A track appeared on the right. Muddy. Grass growing down the center, between the wheel ruts. Ideal.

He turned in, rolling slowly. His compact bumped over the edge of the tarmac and onto the washboard surface. Behind him, the cruiser's light bounced in the same spot.

He kept moving. Easing them deeper into the line of trees and overgrowth.

The cruiser slowed, staying back, perhaps unwilling to be tempted into the dark woods. Luigi considered where the road might lead. Driving the compact, he'd be stranded if he hit a patch of mud. The cops would catch him quickly. An outcome he couldn't accept. For one thing, Enzo would be livid.

The thought made him grin. He'd been making Enzo livid for three decades now and both brothers had the scars to prove it.

Luigi found a solid place and came to a halt. The cruiser moved a few feet closer. Into the edge of the woods. The very edge.

Luigi looked back, he couldn't see into the cruiser. Was there one or two cops in the car? He exhaled. Two. There'd be two. Safer to assume two. No policeman should be out at this time of night on his own.

He cursed the airline security that required him to travel here without a gun. If he'd been to Orlando before, he'd have a gun stashed here as he always did. But this was his first, and he hoped, last visit. He hated the place.

His contingency plans required him to obtain a knife after every flight where a gun wasn't readily available. He was good with a knife. Knives had several advantages. Perhaps the most significant advantage was that unlike guns, he could kill quietly with a knife.

The night before, he'd driven several miles to a big box sporting goods store where he'd purchased two hunting knives with cash. One of the knives was strapped above his ankle, the other tucked between his seat and the center console, the merest tip of the handle protruding above the seat cushion for easy access.

He'd practiced grabbing the handle until he was satisfied he could reach it in a hurry. The police would be armed, and the knife was his last option for dealing with the situation. But if he had to, he wouldn't hesitate.

Blinding light bathed Luigi's rental. He glanced into the rearview mirror. Twin spotlights on either side of the cruiser had been turned on. He squinted. He couldn't even make out the outline of the cruiser any more.

He swore. These guys weren't going to be as easy as he'd thought.

Two officers stepped out of the cruiser. One was heavy, likely a regular at the doughnut stand. The other was thinner, younger. They unclipped their holsters, and loosened their weapons, breaking the friction. Ready.

The thin one stood behind Luigi's rental.

The heavy one walked around to the driver's door. "Wollard" was clearly visible on his metal nameplate pinned to the front of his shirt. He stood a few feet away from the window pointing a long flashlight into Luigi's face.

Luigi took a deep breath, and let it out, relaxing his muscles and installing a calm expression on his face.

Wollard's gun was clearly visible to a casual observer. Several items hung from his belt and the strap that ran diagonally across his chest. Luigi gazed at them all. In the mist, it was hard to tell if any of the accessories held a body camera.

Luigi pressed a button, and lowered his window. He smiled, and thickened his Italian accent. "*Buongiorno.*"

"Where you from?" Wollard said.

Luigi took a breath. He had his story planned. He always did. He'd gone over it, time and time again, until it sounded natural. Practice was the only way to be convincing. He knew. He'd listened to many liars making up stories on the fly. He could always tell.

"*Italiano.*" He poked at his chest with his thumb. "*Italiano.*"

The officer nodded. "You speak English?"

Luigi gestured with his finger and thumb, squeezing them together to indicate he understood a little.

Wollard nodded. "Well, whether you understand me or not, you were speeding through our town. Ran a red light. I'm going to need to see your license."

Luigi raised his eyebrows, and shrugged.

"License," Wollard said.

Luigi nodded. "Ah, *Si, si.*"

He made a performance of rummaging through his pockets before producing an Italian driver's license. It was the one he had used at the rental car counter. It matched his passport. The license and the passport were both genuine, but neither were his.

He wasn't concerned. No authorities would be tracking either because the original owner hadn't declared them lost. Nor would he ever do so. Luigi had made certain of that before he stole the identification.

Luigi held out the dead man's license.

Wollard studied the writing. He used a flashlight and turned the credit-card-sized license over several times. Luigi felt sure the man couldn't read Italian.

Wollard pointed the flashlight in Luigi's face. "What are you doing here?"

Luigi tapped his chest. "Disney. I come...the Orlando...for your Disney."

Wollard stared. "You're alone?"

Luigi raised his eyebrows. "Er..."

The officer sniffed. "Kids. Do you have kids?"

"Er..."

"*Bam-bee-nee?*"

Luigi nodded. He wanted to reach for the knife and skewer the man, but instead he smiled and shook his head. "No, no. *In Italia.*" He held up four fingers. "*Quattro.*"

The thin officer had walked up to the window now and he took the license. Luigi caught the name on his shirt, "Coogan."

He wandered back to his spot behind Luigi, probably using his radio to give Luigi's details to his dispatcher. Good. The search would take a while and keep the dispatcher occupied.

The heavy cop cast his flashlight beam onto the rear seat and shined on the overnight bag. "Where are you staying?"

Luigi shook his head, and shrugged.

"Hotel?" Wollard said.

"*Si, si.* Day-tone-er. Surfside Motel."

Wollard moved his flashlight onto the passenger side of the car. Luigi immediately cursed himself. The plastic bag he'd brought from the motel full of bleach wipes lay in the foot-well, brilliant white in the flashlight's glare.

"What's that?" Wollard said, holding the beam steadily.

"It's..." Luigi struggled for a plausible reason to be carrying the bag's contents in his car.

Wollard opened Luigi's door. "I'm going to have to ask you to step out, sir."

Luigi looked up at the man. Up close, he was even bigger and heavier than he'd seemed when he'd walked in the cruiser's headlights. His belt had pockets and clips that rattled as he moved. His gun protruded from its holster.

Luigi stepped out.

The officer pointed to the front of the car. "Hands on the hood, sir."

Luigi turned, and placed his hands on the car's damp metalwork.

Coogan moved up to the side of the rental, putting Wollard between himself and Luigi. Luigi resisted the temptation to grin. The man was an idiot.

Wollard leaned into the car, reaching for the plastic bag.

Luigi reached over the driver's door, across Wollard's back, and whipped his gun from its holster.

Coogan went for his gun. An awkward twist of his arm. His elbow poking out. His wrist canted backwards. Fractions of a second wasted.

Luigi fired. Two shots. Loud in the night quiet. Coogan jerked backward, arms flailing.

Wollard came up, wrapping his arm around Luigi's and twisting it back.

Luigi rotated, but Wollard held on. The big man raced around the driver's door, his greater weight dragging Luigi in an arc.

Luigi stumbled. Wollard slammed Luigi into the hood. Face down. Arms outstretched.

Luigi's balance swam. Wollard pounded a heavy blow into Luigi's side.

Luigi levered himself upright, and ripped his arm from Wollard's grasp. He clenched his fists, but to his horror the gun was gone.

Wollard sidestepped, keeping Luigi close to the car. Luigi faked right.

Wollard wasn't fooled. He threw a heavy jab, forward and down, using his advantage in height and weight.

The blow hit Luigi on the neck. His head jerked sideways. Pain traveled down his back like an electric bolt. The muscles in his neck spasmed. The side of his head felt like it was on fire.

His knees gave out. He dropped like a stone, leaning backward, his spine scraping down the front of the rental.

Wollard grabbed Luigi's shirt, and drew his right arm back.

Luigi reached for the knife strapped to his ankle. He shoved his knife upward. He gripped hard. Its six-inch blade prone. He barely had to move it.

Wollard lunged. His fist clenched. A giant barreling blow. All of his venom, all of his anger. Sweeping round and down. All his weight bearing down. His feet practically leaving the ground with the effort. Fist, arm, shoulder.

Onto Luigi's knife. It pierced under Wollard's arm. Away from the belts and any protections. Soft flesh. The whole blade. All the way in.

Wollard's arm fell. Tumbling flesh and bone, not the tensed muscles of the instant before. Luigi twisted and rolled, pushing Wollard sideways before his weight fell on him. Wollard collapsed. Luigi forced himself up on his knees.

Wollard cried in pain.

Luigi swept his blade across the man's neck, and the woods fell silent.

His heart pounded. He used the front of the rental car to help himself stand up. He breathed hard, and rubbed the side of his head and neck. Without the knife, the cop could have killed him.

He breathed out hard. The cop didn't kill him. He'd gotten the better of the older, heavier man.

Coogan lay still on the far side of the car, his arms outstretched, and one leg twisted under him. Luigi walked around the car and picked up his gun. He fired three shots into the man's head. Better safe than sorry.

He searched Coogan's pockets and found a set of car keys. In the cruiser, he found the off switch for the spotlights. He went back to his car and turned off his engine and lights. Darkness descended. He checked his watch by the moonlight. He still had time, but he'd have to work fast.

He dragged Coogan into the bushes by the feet, his limp body bumping over rocks. He found Coogan's radio and switched it off.

He patted Coogan down. No body camera, which was the first lucky break Luigi had had since the cruiser's lights flashed in his rearview mirror.

Wollard was far heavier. And bloodier. Pulling him by the feet didn't work. Luigi gripped Wollard's belt, carefully avoiding his blood. He pulled Wollard to the opposite side of the road and rolled his body into the ditch. The heavy cop landed in the stagnant water at the bottom of the ditch with a splash.

The cruiser was parked behind the rental. Luigi couldn't risk backing it out onto the road, even though no one had passed by. He moved his compact forward and half-off one side of the muddy lane. He found his packet of bleach wipes, then drove the cruiser around the compact on the other side of the lane.

Fifty feet down, he turned off. He gunned the engine and embedded the car into the tangled undergrowth. When the tires did nothing but spin, he switched off the engine.

He used the wipes to clean the steering wheel and gearshift. He wiped around the doors. He couldn't open the front two doors because of the undergrowth, so he climbed into the back and out.

He walked to his rental, satisfied the cruiser wasn't visible.

Wollard's flashlight lay on the ground by the compact. Luigi used it to scour the ground for evidence. Dark patches might in time be identified as blood, but Luigi had left nothing behind.

He used the wipes to clean his hands and face. He stripped off his shirt and pants, and stuffed them in the bulging plastic bag. He donned fresh clothes from his overnight bag.

He checked his watch. Time to go. He was twenty-five miles from his destination. No doubt the Grantlys lived in an upscale community. All of these chumps did. Along the way, he would find a dump for the plastic bag, and whatever happened, he would stop at every single red light all the way to Winter Park.

# CHAPTER SIXTEEN

*Winter Park, Florida*
*May 11*

JESS PARALLEL PARKED AT the office of Grantly & Son at the posted 7:00 a.m. opening time. The lights were already on, and a woman occupied one of the big desks, but the sign on the door still read closed.

According to an elegant script over the window, the company had been established in 1945. The plate glass window fronted the main street. Window boxes filled with red geraniums splashed color across the width of the storefront. A thin gold coach line ran around the door and window, contrasting with the rich green paint. The effect reminded Jess of an old-fashioned steam train, solid and reliable.

She locked the SUV, and stood on the sidewalk. It was barely daylight. Faux antique streetlights illuminated the storefronts, and a patchy fog swirled around their beams. The dampness was heavy in the air. Yesterday's rain, evaporated in the afternoon heat, was coming back to earth as this morning's fog.

The smell of fresh bread wafted from a bakery on the corner. It battled the smell of bacon from a diner sitting catty-cornered from the bakery. Her stomach growled. Her early morning coffee had awakened her senses, but not quelled her appetite.

She ducked into the bakery, and bought a selection of breakfast pastries. The sugar and the carbs would buoy Grantly's metabolism. Every little thing would help her push him into revealing his secrets.

Jess returned to Grantly & Son's, and put her phone on silent mode. She wanted no distractions during the interview. The entrance was on the right side of the window. A cheerful bell announced her arrival when she pulled on the polished brass door handle.

The antiques that decorated the small lobby looked as if they might have been original to the business. Incandescent lamps cast a soft glow over the room. An oak desk in the center faced the big window, allowing the receptionist a view of the town.

When so many offices were nothing more than cubicles in high-rise buildings, this one reflected a solid, old-fashioned character of the kind Jess's grandmother would have called breeding.

At the sound of the bell, the woman behind the desk glanced up from her morning paper. She sported a bright fuchsia welcoming smile.

She stood up. "May I help you?" Her voice was high pitched, sing-song, a perky tone that would resonate well on the telephone. She didn't introduce herself and there was no nameplate on her desk. Jess guessed everyone in town already knew who she was. She seemed that type.

Jess smiled and pulled off her sunglasses, hoping the dark

circles under her eyes had faded. "I'm looking for Wilson Grantly."

The woman shook her head. Her smile dimmed, and a deep crease furrowed her brow. "Did you have an appointment?"

The question rang alarm bells in Jess's skull.

She held out the box of pastries. "I was just hoping he might be available."

Miss Fuchsia glanced toward her computer screen. She seemed efficient and polished, and if Jess had an appointment, she was sure Miss Fuchsia would have known about it.

Jess held out her business card. "Jessica Kimball, *Taboo Magazine*."

Miss Fuchsia's eyebrows arched becomingly, and her eyes widened. The lipstick formed a vivid little "Ooo."

Jess had seen the reaction before. A chance for a feature or even a mention in *Taboo* didn't come along every day. Most people didn't squander the opportunity. She smiled. "I'd like to speak to Mr. Grantly."

The woman took the card. She read the glossy front before turning it over to the plain white and back again. "Oh."

Jess frowned. "Is there a problem?"

"No, no." The woman planted the card on her desk. In the middle. Squarely aligned. "I'm sure he would be delighted to talk to you."

Jess exhaled. "Good. I'm working on a big feature. The challenges faced by successful small businesses." She gestured to the office. "Like this one."

The woman looked around as if to assure everything was photo ready.

Jess cleared her throat. "I'm kind of on a tight deadline."

Miss Fuchsia shook her head. "Right. Yes. Well. I'm sure he

would love to speak to you, but…" She bit her lip. "He's not in the office."

"Are you expecting him back?"

Her eyes opened wide. "Oh yes. Perhaps you could…" She took a deep breath. "He'll be so disappointed. I mean if he can't speak to you."

Jess waved the box of pastries. "Well, here I am."

"Yes." Miss Fuchsia pushed her chair back. "But I'm afraid he won't be back for a while. He's in Italy."

Jess's breath snagged and for the second time in as many minutes, alarm bells rang in her head. "Italy?"

The woman nodded. "Rome, in fact."

Jess strained to keep the smile on her face. "How nice."

"Oh, it is." Miss Fuchsia fairly beamed. "I've been looking. On the Internet. It's wonderful. So many places, and—"

"So, he's out of the country."

"Yes. Yes, I'm afraid he is. But I just know he would love to talk to you. About…you know…"

"His business?"

The woman nodded.

Jess sighed. "When did he leave?"

"Last week."

"And when is he returning?"

"Ah, well. He's got an open-ended ticket." She leaned closer to Jess and whispered, "He left it on his desk, and, well…I had to look."

Jess put the pastries on Miss Fuchsia's desk. "Do you know what he's doing in Rome?"

"Vacation. He's taking a vacation." The woman frowned and shook her head. "He's been under a lot of stress lately. Should do him a world of good."

"Maybe."

Miss Fuchsia shifted her weight from one leg to the other. She glanced down at the pastry box.

Jess clenched and unclenched her fists. Italy? Could it be? Had that lying, sniveling so-and-so Blazek been telling the truth for once? Had he really been right? The operation was run by Italians? A cold chill ran down her arms. Or, was Grantly really the kingpin? Alive because he was the one calling the shots? Or the cyanide, in this case.

"Miss Kimball?"

Jess snapped her gaze to Miss Fuchsia's worried face. "Rome. Do you know where he's staying?"

Miss Fuchsia pursed her bright pink lips and shook her head. "Sorry."

"Any way to contact him?"

"He trusts us to run the place." She shifted her weight, shaking her head at the same time. "Perhaps I could answer some questions."

Jess tapped the leg of her sunglasses against her front tooth. Grantly. In Italy. Blazek's claim confirmed by Miss Fuchsia. She rubbed her forehead.

"Enjoy the pastries. You've been very helpful. Thanks." She turned and walked out. The green door. The brass handle. Dawn growing into morning outside when she reached the sidewalk.

She pulled out her phone and dialed Morris.

He answered before it even rang. "You okay?"

She frowned. "Yes. Why?"

"I've been calling and calling."

She glanced at the display on her phone. Seven missed calls. One number. She returned the phone to her ear. "Sorry. Grantly's in Italy."

Morris didn't reply.

"Did you hear me?"

Morris nodded. "Yeah, yeah. Just thinking."

"He's the only one still alive on Blazek's list, and—"

"Wait. Where are you?"

"Outside Grantly's real estate office."

"Alone?"

"Yes."

"People around?"

"Yeah, I'm standing on the sidewalk. Why?"

"Do you feel safe?"

"What the hell are you talking about?"

"Do you have a gun?"

She took a breath for patience. "Glock. Why?"

"Know how to use it?"

"Morris!"

She heard a strong stream of air blowing into his phone before he said, "Guy's name was Marek. We found him."

"Marek?" She frowned. "The man Candace Supko mentioned?"

"One and the same. I called her. Told her you were working with me. She remembered the name, but nothing else."

"So how did you find him?"

"He lived in Canada."

Her skin tingled. "He's dead?"

"Cyanide."

She whistled.

"The scene was staged to look like murder followed by suicide. Like he'd shot his wife, and then killed himself, filled with remorse or rage or whatever."

"But he didn't."

"No."

"How do you know?"

"For one thing, the killer left the kids alive. In a domestic shoot like this, usually the parent kills the kids, too."

Jess said nothing. Her legs felt wobbly. She knew the statistics as well as anyone and Morris was right. But how any parent could kill their own children was always a shock to her.

"Marek owned a nightclub. The Mounties are investigating, but there's plenty of suspicion he was involved in the same type of extortion as Blazek. Maybe even one of the ring leaders." He paused. She heard the satisfaction in his voice when he said, "Marek's wife? Her family name was Zimmer. Originally from New Orleans."

Jess's breath caught in her chest. "Let me guess. She was a budding artist."

"Seems like it. She had a gallery in Montreal. And Mrs. Supko was right. The art is dreadful. Probably used those paintings somehow in the extortion ring or maybe to launder the money."

She nodded, but he couldn't see her, so she said, "And Grantly?"

"Get this. Marek visited Orlando at least twice that we know of. So far."

Jess looked in through the plate glass window to Miss Fuchsia. "Can you link him to Grantly?"

"We're working on it."

"So you're working on the case now?"

He grunted. "One of nine on my overflowing plate. Don't drop out now, Jess."

"No chance of that." She was surprised by the steel in her voice. "But we need something to link Marek to Grantly. He might simply have gone to Disney World. Millions of people do."

"Montreal to Orlando. It's four hours each way."

"So?"

"Each visit, he only stayed an hour and a half."

Jess paced along the sidewalk. "So he met Grantly."

"Most likely, even though we don't have evidence of a meeting. Yet."

"Cameras? At the airport?"

"Still checking. The Mounties think when the scammers have squeezed everything they can from their victims, they use ransom threats."

"Like they're not doing that anyway with the whole scam."

"No, I mean literally. They take a child or a spouse or a girlfriend."

Jess exhaled. She put her hand on her SUV, and leaned forward. Kidnap? Ransom? She breathed hard. Forcing back the mist that was rolling over her. A red mist. Fogging her mind with hot anger.

"Jess?"

She uh-huh'd. She didn't trust herself to say anything else.

"Jess, Wilson Grantly may be the hostage. He might have been operating the scam, or a victim of the scam. Regardless, my guess is he's in trouble."

"It could be anything." She straightened up, shoulders squared. "We've got so little real evidence. Just because Blazek mentioned Italy, and Grantly's gone to Italy, doesn't mean Grantly's in trouble."

"Jess, who goes all the way to Rome for a vacation *alone*?"

"Right." But the urge to tell him a vacation alone in Rome sounded like a wonderful idea almost overcame her.

# CHAPTER SEVENTEEN

*Winter Park, Florida*
*May 11*

LUIGI FICARRA PARKED HIS rental around the corner from the Grantlys' house. He guessed he was a hundred feet away. Closer than he would normally consider prudent, but necessary with the thick fog that concealed everything. He'd checked the forecast. The fog wasn't expected to clear until mid-morning at the earliest.

The clock on the dashboard said 7:09 a.m., but it was still dark, and his body reminded him he'd awakened in the middle of the night. The adrenaline rush from dealing with the cops was wearing off. He stretched and yawned. Even after three days, his jet lag lingered.

He left the engine running. Clouds of vapor billowed from the exhaust, mixing with the fog. He turned up the air-conditioning. The last thing he wanted was for the windows to mist up like the air outside.

He stretched his back. The Grantlys should have been a

simple operation, but nothing seemed easy with them. They had to discuss everything. It was like each of them could only make half a decision. Even when they packed the money, they couldn't decide whether to follow their instructions and pack $100 bills, or just pack what notes they had. Eventually they ran out of time, and packed what they had, and as a result would be carrying more weight than necessary. They were old and stupid, and he would be glad to be rid of them.

Or, he grinned, *get* rid of them. The idea already had great appeal. He'd killed oldsters before. There was not much challenge involved, but killing them was a permanent solution which appealed to him. Surely, at their age it was time for them to go? With their son gone, who would take care of them anyway?

He checked his knives. He took a deep breath. No matter how ready he was to be rid of the Grantlys, he had to be patient. A quarter of a million dollars was at stake.

# CHAPTER EIGHTEEN

JESS LOOKED THROUGH THE door to Grantly & Son. Miss Fuchsia appeared to be busy photocopying. Jess opened the door. The cheerful bell rang, and the woman looked up. "Can I help you? I'm really sorry Mr. Grantly isn't—"

"Look, Rome sounds wonderful, but I don't think Mr. Grantly is there on vacation."

The woman frowned. "He…is. He told me. I mean…why else would he go there?"

"Let me be straight with you. I flew here from New Orleans last night because I think Wilson Grantly is in serious trouble."

Her frown reappeared. A faint line in her makeup suggested it was a frequent visitor. "What kind of trouble?"

"The kind that could put him out of business, or worse."

"What would be worse?" She put her hands over her mouth. "What…what are you saying?"

"You said he trusts you with all aspects of this business. So, you must know if he's got problems."

Jess watched for involuntary signs of confirmation. All she needed was a lead. Morris would handle the rest.

Miss Fuchsia was a professional under pressure. Perhaps a skill learned selling houses. She took her hands from her mouth. "I couldn't possibly comment. I mean, is that what you wanted for your magazine? A scandal? Is that—"

Jess held up her hand, palm out. "Nothing of the sort. But I need to know, has he been short of cash lately? Or had trouble meeting the bills?"

"Well..." She moved from the photocopier to stand behind her desk. "We have postponed some closings lately. Just a little cash flow...I mean—"

"Is his escrow account low? Empty?"

Miss Fuchsia didn't reject the suggestions. She chewed the lipstick off her bottom lip and looked from one side of the office to the other.

Jess waited.

Miss Fuchsia's gaze settled on her desk. She took a deep breath. "Perhaps it would be better if you spoke to Mr. Grantly. Maybe he could help you."

"What?" Jess scowled while her heartbeat galloped. "I thought you said he was in Rome."

"Mr. Grantly. Roger Grantly. Wilson's father."

"His father? Does he know what's going on with the business?"

"He had a heart attack a year ago, so he's semi-retired now. But he worked here every day of his life. He's the only person who, well, could speak on the matter."

If Wilson Grantly was involved in Blazek's extortion ring, Jess figured his father was the last person he would have confessed to, but she had no other option. "Is he here now?"

"No, but he lives nearby. You'll want to be quick, though. They're going to New York today sometime."

"New York?"

"Harriet, that's his wife, she said they've never been. She's a bit more sprightly than he is. Always going on about taking trips and seeing the world." Miss Fuchsia smiled and the mirth reached all the way to her worried brown eyes.

"How old are they?"

"Ninety or so."

"*Ninety?* And they're going to New York alone?"

Miss Fuchsia arched her eyebrows and nodded her agreement, as if she found the idea preposterous, too. "But I'm sure if his son's in trouble, he'd want to know." She scribbled on a post-it and handed it to Jess. "He's a real morning person, you know? Always up early. You wouldn't be waking him. And he makes great coffee. Really nice man. Worked here—"

Jess held up her hand to halt the non-stop chatter. "I'll go talk to him."

Miss Fuchsia sank into her chair. "Right, right. Just a couple of blocks. Five minutes. Less if you're driving. And he's a real morning person. Always was. He—"

"Okay. I'm going."

Miss Fuchsia's professionalism seemed to have deserted her. She stared into the middle distance, unblinking.

"Don't worry, it'll be all right." Jess headed to the door. "Call him now. Tell him I'm on my way. Tell him it's important."

The woman didn't reply. Jess couldn't tell if she'd heard the instructions, but she only had to go two blocks, it wasn't going to make much difference if Miss Fuchsia called ahead or not.

# CHAPTER NINETEEN

*Winter Park, Florida*
*May 11*

LUIGI ROLLED HIS SHOULDERS. The rental car's seats were soft. They seemed to have sunk even lower since he left the cops. American cars were nothing like his beloved Lamborghini.

The mist still swirled in the air, thick and lumpy. The Grantly's house was still on the edge of visibility. A faint light glowed from one of the front rooms, but the old people hadn't stepped out of the door, and they probably wouldn't for some time yet.

The clock showed 7:11. It would be after one o'clock in the afternoon in Italy. A good time to call Enzo.

He pulled his phone from his pocket. The creaky plastic felt slippery in his hands. The screen was dim, the colors washed out. It was the sort of cheap rubbish he hated. At home, he would have thrown it away, but not in the USA.

He'd purchased the disposable phone on a previous trip

and stored it in a rental locker at JFK airport. It was a useful trick he had devised as his trips to the U.S. became more frequent.

Like so many first-world countries, surveillance cameras were mounted everywhere in the U.S., even in the cheapest of convenience stores. Which meant purchasing an identity-less, throwaway phone still carried a significant risk. But the risk was greatly reduced when he'd realized that Americans have short memories. A characteristic that carried over to their surveillance. He smiled. Americans were idiots.

He dialed Enzo. The number his brother was using while Luigi was traveling in the U.S. The phone buzzed with each button press. Fifteen digits. Fifteen toneless buzzes. As was their usual protocol, the number changed frequently. One number per trip stateside. No less. Sometimes, more.

Luigi watched dots travel across the flimsy screen. They rolled off one end of the display, and reappeared on the other. He drummed his fingers on the steering wheel. The dots disappeared, and the display showed "connected."

He held the phone to his ear. He heard three tones. Buttons being pressed on the other end. One long, two short. His brother's signal.

Luigi pressed a button for a couple of seconds. No fanciful tunes for him. With their private coded greeting completed, Luigi spoke.

"I'm waiting outside their place." He didn't elaborate on names. He didn't have to. His brother would know who the Grantlys were.

"Good," Enzo said.

"They took some persuading, though."

"The old ones always do. I'm not sure if it's because they're wiser, or more stupid."

"Trust me, it's definitely the latter." Luigi squirmed in the pillowed seat.

"But it's all under control, yes?"

"What do you think?"

"I have every confidence in you." Enzo sounded preoccupied. Having lunch, perhaps.

"Good. Because I'm down to the final run, tailing them all the way."

"Let's hope that's as difficult as it gets."

Luigi grinned. "You spoil all my fun."

"Fun isn't good for profits."

"But it's good for me."

Enzo snorted. "Don't let your fun get in the way of our business."

Luigi gripped the phone harder. He did not reply. Enzo always needed to act like his older brother. They were no longer children. Would he never stop?

Enzo said, "How can you be sure the Grantlys haven't gone to the police?"

"I have it covered. I've had them under surveillance. I've had their phone bugged." Luigi stretched and squirmed, trying to get comfortable. "They haven't made so much as a sandwich without me knowing about it. They're clean. They're good. No police involved."

Enzo took a deep breath. "And they collected the money?"

"Eventually."

"Eventually?"

Luigi shook his head. "I don't know. They left it until the last minute to pack."

"And that doesn't worry you?"

"They're ninety. It's amazing they can walk, let alone pack a case."

Enzo was silent for a moment. "But you're sure they have the money?"

"Positive, I was forced to listen to them count it." He shook his head in the dark. "Three times."

"You didn't find a way to check?"

"They counted every damn bill. I can tell you it was tedious. Damn tedious. But they're too stupid to have faked it." Luigi's patience for the Grantlys was exhausted long ago. If he was in Italy, he'd simply have killed them already and taken the money with him when he left. Unfortunately, that wasn't an option here.

"Let's hope they're not stupid enough to back out." Enzo swallowed something. The noise was followed by a clink of china.

"I have ways to encourage them."

"Be sure you are careful."

"Have I ever been anything else?"

Enzo paused again. "What about three years ago?"

Luigi frowned. He cupped the back of his neck with his hand. "Three years ago?"

"Is your memory so short you've forgotten Las Vegas already?"

Luigi rolled his eyes. "*Pah*. She was a prostitute."

"And she got you arrested."

"For one night. And not even the whole night."

"You were lucky the damn place was more interested in your money than your life."

Luigi laughed. "You're jealous."

"I need a successful conclusion to our business. This time, and every time."

Luigi clenched his teeth. He hated his brother when he insisted he was the only one interested in their business. He took a deep breath. "Like I said, you're only jealous."

"Of a prostitute?"

"You never met her. Because if you had, you'd be begging her."

"I don't believe you were in any state to appraise her particular skills in any way at all."

Luigi laughed. "Like I said, you're jealous."

"You need to focus on the business. The job."

Luigi nodded. "And what about at your end?"

Enzo grunted. "Taviani?"

"Yeah, spineless Taviani."

"Absolutely no problem. I have him under control."

"I don't trust him. He's slippery."

"Don't I know it? He groveled his way into two extensions."

"His family is the best way to control him."

"I know that, too."

"You've got to wonder how someone as worthless as Taviani could amass a pile of beans, let alone a couple of million."

Enzo grunted. "Be grateful he did."

"We should have screwed him for the whole lot."

"Never. You know my rules." The china clinked again. Perhaps Enzo's favorite white demitasse cup resting on its saucer. "You must leave them hope, or they'll do something desperate. How many times do I have to tell you that?"

"We should have gone harder on him. Taken his daughter. That would have supplied proper motivation."

"Absolutely not. It would have motivated him to go to the police."

Luigi snorted. "You just don't like doing business at home."

"Never do business with family and friends. Remember?"

Luigi laughed. "Who the hell would want to call him a friend?"

"You know what I mean. It's a good rule. We will stick to it in the future."

"Unless we find another lemon with a few million going to waste."

Enzo laughed. "Yeah, that would make a difference."

"So, you're paying Taviani a visit this evening?"

"No."

Luigi frowned. His brother's voice had a smug satisfaction to it.

"But that was the plan."

"It was."

Luigi sighed. "So what now? Don't tell me he begged for a few more days?"

"*Pah*. He would have begged for anything, but I didn't give him a chance."

A faint smile dawned on Luigi's face. "Would have?"

"I had him watched. I knew he had the money. Separate withdrawals, separate banks. Everything below the limit that triggers attention. The whole thing. Just like I told him."

"And?"

"So, I visited him last night. A day early. In case he got cold feet."

Luigi beamed. "He handed it over?"

"I relieved him of the burden."

Luigi pumped his clenched fist close to his chest. "So we're a million better off."

"Nine hundred eighty-five. Fifteen short." Enzo sighed. "He was slippery all the way to the end."

"But who's counting?"

"Me. Every time."

"And Taviani?"

Enzo laughed. "Well…this morning he's all over the news, but last night he was all over the floor. And the walls, and the furniture."

Luigi's smile twisted to one side. "You're a cold one, brother."

"But a rich one."

Luigi nodded. "Yes."

Enzo cleared his throat. "So, get the Grantlys sorted over there, and we can finish things at the airport."

"Count on it. Be ready for my—"

A hundred feet away, two headlights glowed in the mist. Luigi leaned forward, straining to see through the gloom.

"What?" Enzo said.

"Car lights. Outside the Grantly house. I've got to go."

Luigi pressed off, and dropped the phone into the cup holder. It clattered about, cheap plastic bouncing on cheap plastic. He didn't care. He released the handbrake and rolled to within fifty feet of the Grantly house.

The headlights were clear, but the outline of the waiting vehicle was barely visible. He took out one of his knives.

He had no intention of letting anyone disrupt his business with the Grantlys. He turned the knife over. Absolutely no one.

# CHAPTER TWENTY

*Winter Park, Florida*
*May 11*

JESS PULLED UP IN front of a modest bungalow in the town's historic district. Even in the fog, this one was a real estate agent's dream. Gray shingle roof atop a white clapboard exterior trimmed with deep red around the windows. Flower baskets hung on chains around the porch. A snow-white picket fence surrounded the manicured lawn.

She grabbed her bag, and hustled up the steps onto a cypress planked front porch.

She rang the bell.

A brass plate above the door claimed construction in 1925.

Jess studied the number. Nineteen twenty-five? About the same age as the Grantlys. She put her hand on the door. Had one of them been born in the house? Lived at the same address all their lives?

She exhaled. What would that feel like? Did they feel a sense of belonging? Or were they stifled?

She shook her head. She'd never had a permanent home. Nothing long term. Nowhere she had put down roots. All she owned was stuffed into a rented one-bedroom apartment in Denver only because *Taboo Magazine's* corporate offices were there. And she hadn't been back in weeks. She felt zero affection for the place. She could as easily have lived in Nowhereville.

Until she found Peter, she spent as little time as possible inside the same four walls.

She took her hand from the door. What was taking so long? An odd sense of *deja vu* washed over her. For the fourth time in two days, she'd stood outside an unfamiliar door waiting for whatever happened. Would this be the one time she got lucky?

Jess leaned her ear to the door and heard nothing. She pushed the bell again. A series of eight chimes rang out. Then silence returned to the house.

A man walked by on the street. She watched him until he disappeared into the fog, hoping all the time he wasn't part of a neighborhood watch program.

She waited another thirty seconds in case he returned, and then peered through the windows into the Grantlys' living room.

A night-light provided enough illumination to see that the house looked like the set from an old wartime movie. A small sofa. Two winged chairs in a matching, somewhat faded fabric. An oval coffee table. A chest of drawers on spindly legs with ball-and-claw feet.

Jess drummed her nails on the window ledge. The efficient Miss Fuchsia had said Roger Grantly would be home. A real morning person. Great coffee.

Jess bit her lip. He might be all those things, but at ninety-something, he would hardly have decided to take a stroll with his wife through the morning fog. It was barely daylight and the fog was still heavy enough to eat with a spoon.

Jess stepped back from the window. Miss Fuchsia had said something else, too. A heart attack. Last year. Jess breathed. If he knew his son was involved in extortion—maybe even murder—that could certainly be a lot of stress on an old heart.

She put her hand on the doorknob, and turned. The door creaked open. Even in this picturesque town, leaving doors unlocked couldn't be a common practice.

The hair on the back of her neck prickled. Too many people had died already. If his heart had given out, well, there might be nothing she could do to help, but she couldn't turn away.

She pushed open the door. "Mr. Grantly? Are you home?"

The door opened into a hallway with a parquet floor. Large arches led off to the living room on one side and a dining room on the other. The house smelled like a museum that had been liberally coated in furniture polish. An old grandfather clock ticked like a metronome, but there were no voices.

She stepped into the house, and closed the door behind her. The wood floor clicked under her shoes. She cleared her throat.

"Mr. Grantly?" She turned her head, listened for the faintest sound of movement, but heard nothing. "Mrs. Grantly?"

She looked through the arch into the living room. The cushions on the chairs were plumped and upright. The coffee table was empty except for a large hardback book with a jungle picture on the cover. A television remote was balanced on the arm of a chair.

But no one in the room.

She passed the grandfather clock. It was a minute from 7:30. The parquet creaked under her shoes. "Mr. Grantly?"

No answer.

She looked around the edge of the arch into the dining room, and jerked back. Facing her across the room, a full-sized suit of armor stood at attention. The armor had a moveable cover for the face, but it had been lifted, leaving a dark gaping hole where the knight's eyes should have been.

She studied the armor for a moment, fully expecting it to walk toward her, but like everything else she'd seen in the house, it wasn't alive. She regretted the thought the moment it popped into her head. She bit her lip. She took a deep breath, and turned away from the dining room.

Winchester chimes rang out, strident, reverberating off the wooden floor. Jess's heart jumped. She lurched away from the grandfather clock. The hammers banged on. Tones evenly spaced. Her heartbeat synced to each one. She took a deep breath. Seven thirty.

As the last tone faded, she realized the chimes were abnormally loud. Which probably meant at least one of the Grantlys had to be deaf because no one with normal hearing could possibly sleep through that racket.

She looked down the hallway. Sleep? The Grantlys couldn't possibly still be asleep, could they? Her skin tingled. If they weren't out walking and they weren't responding to her voice, there weren't many other good reasons she could think of for their failure to acknowledge her presence in their home.

The far end of the hall had no window. It grew darker the farther it went into the house. Thin lines of light escaped underneath the remaining doors.

She drew her gun, and moved down the hallway. The air changed. The waxy museum smell gave way to a heavier scent. Chicken, perhaps? Or beef? She bit her lip. Or perhaps something else.

The next door was open a fraction. Through the gap, she saw

a kitchen stove, and heard the hum of a refrigerator. She put her hand on the doorknob, and froze.

Behind her, something clicked. A loud, metallic click with a crunching noise. It was almost like the ratcheting of a shotgun. She swallowed. She adjusted her grip on the Glock, and turned.

There was no one behind her. Light reflected from the polished wood floor. The front door was closed, just as she had left it.

A muffled voice drifted through the house. She spun back and forth, training the gun up and down the hallway. From light to dark and back again. She saw no one.

She heard the voice again. Quiet. Indistinct. It could be the Grantlys. Perhaps she had scared them, walking into their house. Then again, why hadn't they responded to the doorbell, or her shouts?

She took a deep breath. There was only one answer, and she didn't like it.

The voice didn't belong to either of the Grantlys.

She stepped to the next door. Moving slowly. Lifting the heel of her shoe before the toe. Placing the heel down first. Gently shifting her weight from foot to foot. She kept her mouth open to keep her breathing silent.

The voice stopped.

She paused outside the door, and eased herself lower to become a smaller target.

The voice started again. A few words. Still quiet. Still muffled.

She tightened her grip on her Glock, and placed her left hand on the door. Another word drifted through the air.

She took a deep breath, held it in her lungs, and looked at the doorknob.

Twist and push. That was all she had to do. Twist hard, and push hard. Nothing half-hearted. No rattling the door. No advance warning.

She twisted and pushed. Punching the door inward, holding her gun forward, her gaze sweeping the room.

It was a bedroom. An empty bedroom.

The voice sounded again. Mumbled and muffled, and coming from the corner of the room. She released the breath she'd been holding and stood up, feeling a little relieved and a little silly.

In the corner was a bedside table, a woman's robe lying across it. She picked up the robe. A clock radio perched on the table underneath the summer weight fabric. A talk show host interviewing some politician. The alarm was set for seven thirty, and the clock was running a little slow.

She pressed the power button, and the radio made the same crunching, ratcheting shotgun sound as it turned off. She shook her head. Who would want to wake up every morning to that?

Jess placed the robe on the bed. The situation was still confounding. The Grantlys had set an alarm to wake them at seven thirty, yet they weren't in their beds?

She glanced around the room. The same wartime style of furniture crowded the floor. A full sized four-poster bed snugged up against one wall. Bulky oak furniture lined the other walls, leaving very little empty floor space.

Several framed photographs rested on the dresser. One posed portrait of an elderly couple seated in the living room with a younger man standing behind them was dated the previous year. Roger and his wife with their son, Wilson, presumably.

Two similar photos, taken in prior years, included younger versions of the three along with another man who resembled

Mrs. Grantly. A second son, perhaps. Younger than Wilson. Miss Fuchsia hadn't mentioned that Wilson had a brother. One thing seemed out of place in the old-fashioned room. A small painting hanging near the closet. Childish. Brightly colored swatches made with a wide brush on a white canvas. Jess moved to get a closer look at the artist's signature. Zimmer. Again.

She pulled out her phone and took pictures.

She stood and scanned the room. Nothing seemed amiss. The furniture was organized. Shelves were dusted, *tchotchkes* artfully arranged. There were no signs of any disturbance.

She walked out into the hall. "Mr. Grantly!" she shouted and then waited and shouted again. "Mrs. Grantly!" No response.

She ducked in and out of another bedroom, a bathroom, and finally stepped into the kitchen.

A large stove dominated one wall. There was a dishwasher, but no microwave. The fridge sported a few business cards and notes adhered to it with magnets.

A bell rang, like an old-fashioned phone. Her heart slammed. She whipped her gun around. Her mouth fell open and she clamped it shut.

A black Bakelite phone was mounted on the wall. She blinked. She'd never seen the first plastic phones except in old movies. This one seemed to be working.

The bell rang again. She breathed in and out.

She was way too jumpy. What did she expect? A couple of ninety-year-olds to pop out and attack her? She wagged her head and smiled. Her heart calmed and her breathing evened out, too.

An old answering machine picked up. A radio announcer's voice started. Rounded tones, lower octaves, each word precisely enunciated. "You've reached the Grantly residence. Harriet and I aren't here at the moment. Leave a message, and we will call you back soon. Wait for the beep."

Roger Grantly. Curiously, his voice carried no trace of a southern accent. Surprising for a man who was born and raised and lived all his life almost as far south as one could get without leaving the country.

The answering machine tape kept rolling a second or two before Miss Fuchsia's voice came from the machine's speaker. "Mr. Grantly? Harriet? Are you there? Please pick up. There is a woman who wants to get in touch with Wilson. Please—"

Jess grabbed the receiver off the wall. It was huge, and surprisingly heavy. "This is Jess Kimball. Mr. and Mrs. Grantly aren't here."

Miss Fuchsia gasped. "Aren't there? But…how'd you get inside?"

"The door was unlocked."

"Really?"

"I thought they might be in trouble, so I let myself in. But there's no one here."

"In trouble? I thought you said it was Wilson Grantly in trouble."

"It's not even eight o'clock in the morning, and a pair of ninety-year-olds aren't at home? I'd say that's a little unusual, wouldn't you?" Jess raked her fingers through her hair and held onto her patience.

Miss Fuchsia's rapid, shallow breathing came across the phone line. "I can call the car service to confirm, but perhaps they left for the airport."

"You said they were leaving today."

"Yes."

"Before eight o'clock?"

"Maybe. I just assumed it'd be later. They can't have left that long ago."

"Do you have their cell phone number?"

"Oh, no. They're not that technical." Miss Fuchsia laughed. "They never understood why people needed a phone with them all the time. Wilson had to help them set up the answering machine and they were twenty years younger back then."

"Do you know what flight they're booked on?"

"No."

"Then can you check with the car company and get back to me on my cell? It's important."

Miss Fuchsia "uh-huh'd," and hung up.

Jess settled the handset back on the phone's cradle, and looked at the notes stuck to the fridge door. She scanned the tidy papers pressed to the surface by cutesy cat magnets, and pulled off a handwritten note. It listed dates and flight times for Orlando and New York.

There was one more flight listed on the note. Jess's blood ran cold when she saw it. She leaned heavily against a kitchen cabinet.

Roger and Harriet Grantly had tickets for Rome.

# CHAPTER TWENTY-ONE

JESS LOOKED AT THE handwritten note and swallowed. The letters were carefully formed. The A's were rounded, the E's had straight horizontal lines, not the looping swirl of many styles.

The writer had taken care with the presentation. It was something important to them. Something they wanted to ensure was correct, not open for misinterpretation.

But the wobble in the lines was clear, the l's and t's in particular. An old and unsteady hand, but a determined and careful one.

Jess read the dates and airport names for a second time. The Grantlys' flight wasn't scheduled to depart from Orlando International Airport for several hours. More than enough time for most people, but maybe a challenge for a pair of ninety-year-olds.

She looked around the house. Even with this schedule, they should still be home. They'd left for the airport very early. Miss Fuchsia was right that they were traveling to New York today, but she was thinking from a younger person's mindset. Older people who didn't fly often would want plenty of time to account for any possible problems. They definitely wouldn't want to miss the flight and be forced to reschedule this particular trip.

She locked the front door, and thumbed through the contact list on her phone while she jogged off the porch and through the garden, back to the rental. The SUV's leather seats were hot. She tossed the keys into the cup holder, thankful for the vehicle's pushbutton start. The engine burst into life, and the air-conditioning pushed a stream of tepid air into the cabin.

A picture of the SUV rotated on a big display in the middle of the dashboard. She tapped her foot as she waited for it to finish its egotistical pirouette, and stabbed the button marked "phone" as soon as it appeared.

A list of her recent calls ran down the display. She didn't have to search far back to find Morris's number. As she reached to press the option to call him, the words "Incoming Call" appeared. She punched "Accept" and Miss Fuchsia's voice tumbled breathlessly from the speakers like a waterfall.

"You were right. They only left home about ten minutes ago. They've gone to the airport. Definitely. The car service got a call from Mr. Grantly last night. He asked to go earlier. They've taken them already. To Orlando. International—"

"Okay. Calm down. I'm on the way to the airport now. They're only a few minutes ahead of me. I'll catch up with them."

"You will be able to help them, won't you? And Mr. Grantly? I mean, Wilson?"

"I'll do my best."

"Should...should I call the police? They could—"

"I'm going to call the FBI, right now, after we hang up."

"Oh! The FBI? Is that…necessary?"

"I've got to go…Miss…Miss. I have to go. Don't worry."

Jess didn't wait for the woman's reply before severing the call.

Morris's number reappeared on the display. She fastened her seatbelt, and pulled into the travel lane while the ringing tone pulsed.

A navigation screen appeared in a corner of the display. She chose the "Rental Car Return" option, and began following its directions from Winter Park to the Orlando airport. Her third airport in less than twenty-four hours. She remembered the days when she was desperate to fly anywhere and everywhere. When she was a kid. Before she got pregnant at sixteen and her childhood ended.

Morris picked up the call. "Can I help you?" he said, curtly, as if her call was a nuisance and he hadn't practically strong-armed her into helping him less than twelve hours ago.

"Sounds like you are not alone," she guessed, although she didn't hear any noises suggesting a crowd on his end.

"Right."

"Can't talk now?"

"Exactly."

The navigation system prompted her to take the next turn for the on-ramp to the highway. She barely saw the sign in the heavy, drifting fog. Not the shortest route to Orlando International, but it was the fastest, given the early morning rush hour traffic and the poor visibility. She could make up the time lost to the Grantlys' head start. Maybe.

She took a deep breath, "Here's the highlights. Wilson Grantly's secretary says he's in Rome on vacation."

"I know. You said."

"She saw the ticket, so we know that for sure."

"Having a ticket isn't the same thing as being there."

"Maybe, but his parents told her they were going to New York."

She heard tapping on his end of the line.

"I don't get it," he said.

"What they didn't tell the secretary was that they're also going on to Rome."

"How do you know that?"

"There was a note on their refrigerator."

"You've talked to them?"

"No. They'd left for the airport ten minutes before I got to their house."

"Sooooo." He sighed. "How did you get the note?"

"The front door was open."

He groaned. "Hang on a second." She heard a thump, as if he'd put his hand over the phone, and then his muffled voice said, "I'm going to have to take this call."

He was back a moment later. "Kimball, this is an FBI investigation. A law-abiding investigation. Not because criminals obey the law, but because if we don't, we have nothing we can use in front of a judge. No justice for victims. Remember?"

"I know that." If he'd been sitting in the SUV next to her, she might have punched him.

"So, you can't go breaking and entering."

"I didn't. I told you. The front door was open."

"Jess, who leaves their front door open in this day and age?"

"Ninety-something year olds?"

"Ninety…"

She could almost hear the gears turning in Morris's head.

"Grantly and Son was established in 1945." She explained the situation he should already have figured out. "Even if Grantly senior was twenty way back then when his dad started the business, he's ninety at least."

Morris whistled.

"Look, we don't have time for chatter right now." Jess peered ahead through the fog. "According to the note, they're departing from the Orlando airport to catch a flight to New York and then to Rome."

She was driving west, so the blinding sunrise was behind her, off and on, when it wasn't obscured by fog. Traffic was still moving at the speed limit, or maybe a bit more.

"I can get the passenger manifests," Morris offered. "Are you heading to the airport?"

"Hell, yes." Jess swerved to avoid merging traffic from the right and moved the SUV two lanes left into the fast travel lane. "Based on everything we know, Wilson Grantly is probably being held for ransom, and his ninety-year-old parents think they're going to pay the money and get him back."

"Jesus," he said.

"Eloquently put, but we need something a bit more constructive."

"Wait a minute."

There was silence on the line. Jess settled into an eighty-mile-an-hour cruise, keeping up with traffic but as far above the speed limit as she felt comfortable with given the weather conditions. Vehicles ahead of her were moving at a good clip, and at least a couple of them had passed her like she was standing still.

A few seconds later, Morris came back on the line. "We can't detain them. No legitimate reason to. They've done nothing wrong as far as we know."

"The note? The information from the Mounties? They lied to the secretary—"

"The note we probably can't use because of the way it was obtained and it doesn't say anything anyway. There's no law against air travel. The Mounties are golden, but we have no provable link for any of the crimes to Grantly, and the secretary...forget about it."

"We have to be able to do something."

"It wouldn't help us stop these guys even if we did detain the Grantlys. The thieves would know. They'd just fold up and move on."

"We have to get to the source of the extortion ring."

"The Grantlys are the only chance we've got."

"Get me a seat."

"Where?"

"On the flight. Same one as them. First class."

"Have to be coach. No government servant flies first class."

"*Taboo* will pay."

He sighed. "You think you can get anything from those two on a plane flight?"

"Get me three seats. Me and them. In a line. Across the aisle. I can move them up after takeoff. Spoil them. Soften them up."

"You sure *Taboo's* going to pay?"

"Just do it, Morris. I'd have my assistant handle it, but Mandy's still asleep. It's early in Denver." She swiped her fingers through her hair and grabbed the wheel again. "I can get it covered. It's our best chance. Hell, it's our only chance."

"I'll get things sorted out." He exhaled loudly. "The tickets will be waiting for you."

"One more thing." She knew he wasn't going to like it. "I've got my Glock. Make sure TSA doesn't hassle me about my gun in my checked bag."

A long pause. Guns and airplanes didn't go well together. Especially if the gun belonged to a civilian. The rigmarole to check her gun through security could take an hour at best, worse if some new recruit handled the paperwork. She had neither the time nor the patience for the process today.

Morris was focused on something else. "Leave it at the airport. Get a locker."

"No."

"I can get the Glock back to you later."

"No."

She could tell she had his full attention when he said, "Jess—"

"An hour ago, you were the one concerned about my safety. Remember Marek? And Kowalski? Now I'm concerned. Fully concerned."

Morris blew out a long stream of air. "Orlando had more guns confiscated from carryon luggage than any other Florida airport last year. Their security is as sensitive as it gets."

"Which is why you've got to solve the problem before I get there. I'm about fifteen minutes away."

Silence.

"Look, I don't want to be caught up with the TSA. I'll check my bag with the gun in it. I'm not asking to take it aboard with me. But I don't have time for any crap. Just fix it, or I'm going to lose the Grantlys." He didn't jump in with approval, so she said, "They're your only viable lead in this case. Is that what you want? Kiss them goodbye and hope for the best?"

"You're a civilian, Jess. I'm not even sure I should be—"

"Do it, Morris. Two-way street, remember? You agreed.

And besides, I'd rather be taking a day off instead of chasing down thieves and killers. That's your job, not mine."

"That is exactly what I'm thinking. We've been treading a fine line between assisting and putting you at unacceptable risk. It's my ass if anything happens to you."

"Fine by me. So can you get someone to the airport? To interview them?" She exhaled and paused to let him work through his own objections. "You think a pair of ninety-year-olds who are so determined to save their son they're traveling all the way to Rome to do the job themselves are going to break down and talk to the FBI? Seriously? You think that?"

"I'll get your tickets and your seat assignments." He sighed and she could hear the surrender in his tone.

"And find out if Wilson Grantly actually took that flight to Rome."

"It's on my list."

# CHAPTER TWENTY-TWO

LUIGI FICARRA WAS FIVE cars behind the Grantlys. He'd been relieved when he realized the car parked in front of their house in the fog was their limo. They must have brought the pick-up time forward. He scoffed. Old people were way too cautious.

The limo moved more slowly than the general flow of freeway traffic. Overtaking the Grantlys should have been easy. But the fog and rush hour made conditions more difficult.

He knew precisely where they were headed, but with the Grantlys, he'd learned never to rely on anything. He'd watched and warned them for several days now. But he didn't trust them to do as they'd been told. Or even to act sensibly.

Could they be trying to trick him? He smirked. He didn't need a reason to kill Wilson Grantly right now. But if his parents wanted to supply an excuse, Luigi would gladly convey the message to his brother.

He kept as tight a distance between his sedan and theirs as

possible, but he was too far back. Luigi moved up one car length at a time whenever he could find a gap. He was a good driver. He'd learned on the streets of Rome and Tuscany where aggressive tactics were not only desirable, they were necessary.

After a few miles, he saw his opening.

He swerved left into the fast travel lane between two oversized vans and back right into a center lane between an eighteen-wheeler and a subcompact and another right to second center between two motorcycles.

Luigi continued to weave in and out of small traffic gaps in each of the travel lanes until he could once again see the Grantlys' limo several car lengths ahead. The driver was holding a stable speed and running in the second center lane closest to the right shoulder. Luigi saw his bumper from time to time. Not quite good enough. He needed to leapfrog one car closer.

An oversized pickup truck blocked the lane in front of him. On his left was a white Mini with a lumbering RV right up on the Mini's rear bumper. The Mini slowed as it entered a thicker patch of fog.

Luigi peered over at the Mini. All he saw were lights that looked like milky blobs lost in the swirling water droplets. The fog thinned. He saw the space in front of the Mini too late. It would have been the ideal moment for him to overtake the Mini, but the little car darted forward into the gap, the driver no doubt spooked by the bulky RV in the rearview mirror.

Luigi checked in the direction of the Grantly's limo. He could barely see it up ahead. The Grantlys could leave the freeway and be gone before he could react.

The situation was unacceptable.

He looked left at the Mini again. The RV was mere feet from its tail.

The fog was getting thicker.

The Mini was slowing.

A gap was opening up. Not big enough for his rental, but good driving was all about being bold.

He cut the steering wheel sharply left in front of the Mini.

The Mini braked hard, tires squealing, enlarging the gap.

Luigi shot into the growing space, stamped on the accelerator to pass the pickup, and swerved back into the middle lane. The Grantlys' limo was clearly visible. They wouldn't get away from him now.

Behind, he saw headlights dancing, swerving, and sliding in the fog. He snorted and then laughed. Idiots that hadn't learned to drive. Fools and amateurs, struggling in the fog. A danger to themselves and everyone else. But he didn't care. The vehicles and their inept drivers were lost to the world behind him, and in moments he forgot all about them.

# CHAPTER TWENTY-THREE

JESS LEANED FORWARD, HER eyes wide, staring out of the SUV's windshield into the heavy, swirling fog. She'd driven hard. Weaving through gaps. Making headway using the constant repetition of mirror, signal, and maneuver.

Good progress in rush hour traffic, and faster than a limo, surely? But she ran out of luck as she came up behind an ocean-liner-sized RV. The big vehicle was charging hard, and the lane to the inside was nose-to-tail. She was stuck.

The fog grew thicker, an almost solid white out, like a Denver blizzard.

She eased back and reduced speed as much as she dared.

The RV's red taillights fishtailed ahead as it braked hard in the fast lane of the interstate. The rear of the vehicle weaved across its lane. The driver was losing control.

Jess gripped the steering wheel at nine and three, elbows wide, muscles clenched, feet hard on the brake pedal with all her weight. The SUV shook, the ABS pulsing the brakes.

The RV's red lights loomed larger. She was gaining on the monster.

She glanced right, and jerked the wheel, diving for a gap in the next lane. The car in front of her there was braking hard, too.

She took her foot off the brake, and wrenched the wheel right again.

The rental speared forward through a brief gap in traffic in the slow lane, across onto the hard shoulder.

The SUV swayed and bumped and planed, but held upright until the tires gripped the grassy edge of the pavement.

She kept the SUV moving, keeping pace with the vehicles swaying and braking to her left, and staying off a concrete retaining wall to her right that guarded a steep downward bank. The RV was way off in the fog.

An eighteen-wheeler emerged from and disappeared back into the mist.

Steel collided ahead, beside, and behind her in an ever-lengthening pileup.

Glass burst.

The sound of screeching tires was punctuated with the sickening pounding, slamming, crunching of metal. Drivers who were half a second less alert than her were paying the price for inattention.

The concrete guardrail to her right ended abruptly. She brought the rental to a stop parallel to the pavement, but angled downward on the steep grassy bank beside the road.

Jess's chest heaved with ragged breaths. Her heart pounded as if it might break through her ribs. Her hands clutched the steering wheel so tightly she saw white knuckles and felt clawed fingers frozen into position while her arms vibrated with tension.

Her legs were fully extended, both feet still pressing the brake pedal against the floor.

She'd been lucky. Her seatbelt held.

The top-heavy SUV had not rolled over. She hadn't been hit.

And she wasn't sandwiched by the colliding vehicle train in the chain reaction collision now choking all westbound lanes of the interstate.

A lone wheel came toward her from the twisted wreckage ahead and flew past, a bouncing loping gait. A thirty-mile-an-hour cartoon stalwart that could kill. It hit the guardrail. A glancing blow that separated a football-size chuck of concrete.

She had to move. Now.

*Get out! Get out!*

She may have screamed the words aloud.

Through sheer force of will she pried her death grip from the steering wheel, threw the transmission into Park, and stopped the engine.

Her phone lay in a cup holder. She fumbled picking it up. Her hands shook. Her fingers disobeyed her simple instructions.

The phone's plastic slipped from her grip, leaping upwards. She swatted at it with her hands, brought it to rest, embraced against her chest, pinned down with her arms. She slid it down into her bag, and felt to confirm her Glock remained nestled securely in its interior pocket.

Confident she had her weapon, she slid across the seats. She shouldered the door open and staggered out on the marginally safer side of the SUV.

The grassy slope on the side of the freeway was steep and rough. She slipped and fell and scraped the skin off her arm before she pushed herself upright again.

The cacophony from the multicar pileup assaulted her ears.

Vehicles were still slamming into each other, caroming across the lanes and onto the shoulders and medians like billiard balls after opening break.

She ran from the SUV before it was added to the pileup.

Twenty feet, forty feet, fifty feet, constantly glancing back over her shoulder, fearing heavy metal heading to mow her down. The more distance she put between her and destruction, the better.

At seventy-five feet, she felt a wave of heat. She looked back, and saw the SUV on its roof, rolling down the steep embankment, flames pouring from the rear. A barely recognizable pickup truck flopped sideways where her SUV had been.

She kept running toward an exit a hundred yards ahead. She slipped on the graveled shoulder and fell twice more. Her hands were scraped and embedded with small stones. Pavement had scrubbed skin from her forearm in a burning rash.

Emergency vehicles raced in the opposite direction, speeding up and onto the interstate using the exit ramp.

She ran on.

Flashing lights zoomed past. Yellow, red, blue, and white. Wailing sirens added to the noise.

She reached the intersection at the base of the exit ramp and staggered to a stop. She fell back against a telephone pole, sweat-soaked, breathing hard, every inch of her nervous system vibrating.

Battered, bruised, scraped, bleeding, and limping.

But alive.

So far.

Emergency vehicles weaved through the chaos. Firefighters arrived to contain blazes. A helicopter, invisible in the fog, circled overhead.

She worked to slow her breathing. She wiped her forehead with her sleeve to soak up the sweat on her face.

She was outside the danger zone, but should she go back? She had extensive training in emergency first aid. Maybe she could help. If she could help, she should.

Her skin felt cold and clammy through the thin fabric of her shirt. A smattering of blood mixed with sweat on her sleeve. She patted herself down and found nothing broken.

She was shaky, but okay. She had to go back.

She pushed herself away from the telephone pole.

Her legs wobbled and her knees buckled. She fell back against the pole, its rough iron surface scraping at her side.

She took a deep breath. "You're okay, Jess," she said aloud.

Her hands trembled. She was weak, she had clammy skin, and her breathing was rapid. Classic signs of mild shock. She'd had it before. It would pass. She took long slow breaths. Deep draughts to get oxygen into her bloodstream.

She breathed and eased herself away from the pole, one foot in front of the other. Small steps. Her knees balancing her weight. She put her hand on the pole.

There was no way she would be able to run back up the ramp. If she did, one of the first responders would probably end up with another patient. Or she'd make it back there, but couldn't help.

The entire scene was in chaos. Flashing lights were everywhere, some visible, some pulsing deep in the fog. Emergency personnel were on scene. Two ambulances were weaving their way through the carnage to provide assistance where it was most needed.

She shook her head. She would be no help to anyone. The professionals needed to triage the situation unobstructed.

She wanted to call Morris, but what good would it do? They had their plan, and she needed to do her part. If she didn't make it to the flight, no one else would be able to help the Grantlys. She knew immediately where she was needed most.

Across the side road, a bus was waiting at a traffic light as emergency vehicles drove through. From the road it was on, it should be heading in the direction of the airport.

She stumbled across the grass and a three-lane road and reached the next stop. She collapsed onto a hard plastic seat under the bus shelter's awning.

Her legs trembled. She breathed hard, trying to regain control of her muscles.

A few minutes later, the bus pulled up. She had no idea where it was headed, but anything was better than walking. She got on.

The bus driver frowned at her. "Honey, you okay?" He leaned forward, looking into her face. "You don't look so good. Not gonna faint, are ya?"

She shook her head. Her body rocked back and forth. She stopped moving her head. "I'm okay. Thanks." Her voice sounded shaky. "The airport?"

The driver nodded and pointed to the price posted on a board.

She dug into her bag, found the fare, and pushed it into his hand. She moved deeper into the bus. The air-conditioning washed over her face as she passed the vents. It felt good.

She worked her way, handhold to handhold, along the tops of the seats until she reached an empty bench and collapsed onto it.

She sat quietly, controlling her breathing, and waiting for the cool air to return her body temperature to normal. Her pulse slowed. The tremors lessened along her limbs.

She held her hands out. The right was steady, the left twitched, still not under her control. She was getting better, but she wasn't right yet.

Her phone buzzed with a message from Morris. He'd secured seats from Orlando to New York on Skyway Airlines Flight 1804. He'd also booked the two extra seats in first class for the Grantlys to sit across the aisle next to her. He said nothing about the last leg of the trip from New York to Rome on Skyway Flight 12 at midnight.

At least as important to Jess, he had cleared her to transport her gun via the curbside check-in desk without scrutiny. A blessing in itself.

Flight 1804 didn't depart for another few hours. Plenty of time to reach Orlando airport, prepare for the trip, and get herself cleaned up.

She couldn't skip on the cleaning up, either. She needed to look respectable for the airport security people, so they didn't get suspicious and awkward with her gun. And she needed to look human to have any hope of getting the Grantlys to talk to her.

She settled into her seat, and let her head drop back. She closed her eyes, making every effort to relax. Once her heart stopped slamming like a bongo drummer, Jess began to formulate a new plan.

# CHAPTER TWENTY-FOUR

*Orlando, Florida*
*May 11*

LUIGI RACED FROM THE rental car bus into the Orlando International Airport terminal. He'd had to abandon his surveillance of the Grantlys to return the rental car. He couldn't dump it. The rental car companies required credit cards to hire their vehicles, and even though his card was stolen, he did not want to take the risk that something might trace it back to him before he was out of the country.

But that wasn't his concern right now. Returning the car meant the Grantlys had been out of his sight for more than thirty minutes. He walked the full length of the terminal, but there was no sign of them, which was probably a good thing. Maybe it meant they had progressed through security.

He had checked in online at the hotel last night with his false identity. His documents were examined briefly before he boarded a tram that carried passengers from the main terminal to the gate.

*It would be almost effortless to bomb the Orlando International Airport*, Luigi thought as he strolled a suitable distance behind the other passengers.

He was bored.

The Grantlys were the last of Marek's clients. Before Enzo terminated him, Marek had chosen the Grantlys because they were exploitable. Easy money. Likely to go all the way.

Marek liked everything to run smoothly right up until the end.

Luigi craved a more capable adversary.

Even while he'd hidden the untraceable .22-caliber Smith & Wesson 22A pistol in the locker and added the key to the others on his key ring, he'd noticed that yes, years after the airplane bombs hit New York City and billions of dollars were spent for increased security measures, the central terminal building here was absurdly vulnerable to a reasonably clever and mildly determined terrorist.

*Imagine what a well-trained terrorist could do.*

The idea intrigued him. Perhaps he'd do it himself one day. Easy work was boring. Suitable for old men like Marek and Enzo. But Luigi craved more excitement.

Perhaps he'd take another trip to Karachi next week. District East was the best although both hunters and prey worth hunting were plentiful everywhere in the city. Executing unarmed people on the busy streets was one of the games he particularly enjoyed.

His chest swelled with pride when he recalled that he'd contributed at least fifty kills last year, Karachi's deadliest year ever. Almost 3,000 total killed in the city.

Still, he could do better. Maybe he could contribute at least one hundred kills this year. He could do it if he spent a little more time and focused on feeble targets. Beggars on the streets were easy to pick off in groups. Children were the hardest to kill because they darted about unpredictably. Others were targets of opportunity. A woman with her back turned. A pair of old men arguing.

Yes, target selection was the key to improving his performance.

Of course, the game would have been more exciting if local authorities weren't so inept. He shrugged. Can't have everything.

He passed a television reporting an 84-vehicle chain reaction crash on the interstate. The news copter footage showed an area Luigi had driven through on his route here from Winter Park. He thought he recognized the mini. Hadn't it been traveling behind him?

He shrugged. Traffic would be tied up for hours. He was lucky the Grantlys had decided to arrive so early this morning after all. Otherwise, they'd have missed the flight.

God is good, as Enzo would say. Luigi's brother was a religious man. Luigi wasn't quite so sure.

The boarding pass he'd printed downstairs and his false identification were briefly examined before he entered the tram that carried passengers from the main terminal to the gate. He'd pick up his Italian passport where he'd stashed it in New York before boarding Flight 12 to Rome.

The electric tram ran smoothly to the airside area. It was a circular pod building for processing passengers where planes were parked nose first at the gates, while their tails protruded like spokes on a wheel. The tram stopped, the doors slid open, and the passengers exited to line up at a physical security checkpoint.

Luigi joined a long, winding queue of passengers backed up in front of him at the tram's exit, engaged in the elaborate and worthless security game that apparently made Americans feel safer. The Italians, the Israelis. *They* knew how to screen passengers. Luigi shrugged. No matter. After tonight, he wouldn't be back in this country for a good long time.

He stood eleven passengers behind the Grantlys in the winding line that reminded him of Euro Disney. He comforted himself with thoughts of success and greater wealth. The Grantlys showed no signs of failure or desire to fail so far. He relaxed into the patience his business required.

*Almost finished.*

From twenty feet ahead, Harriet Grantly turned around and looked at the long line of passengers behind her. Briefly, her saucy blue eyes touched his face. He brought his right hand up to obscure her view, pinched his nose at the bridge with his thumb and forefinger, and tilted his head down as he did so.

Neither of the Grantlys had met him yet. He didn't want her to notice him too soon.

Thank God Americans are so gullible and altruistic. Otherwise, Luigi and his family would have been bankrupt long ago. As it was, since Marek's share would also be included, profits would increase by 300 percent this year alone. Yes, Americans made the best clients, to be sure.

When he glanced up, Harriet had turned toward the front of the winding line of passengers, chatting with a family in front of her. The Grantlys would arrive in New York and fly to Rome with the final installment payment. When they reached Rome, it was only a short ride to the estate in Tuscany.

But he didn't care about security. All he cared about was the Grantlys and their money. Almost a quarter million dollars. With the favorable exchange rate in Italy, it would buy a few trinkets. It wasn't as much as he'd like, but it was easily taken. And the money should be his. He'd worked hard enough for it.

The only logistical problem was removing it from the country. The risk was first in carrying anything through security. If the money was found, there was no practical means of escape.

Which meant that the best method for moving large amounts of cash out of a country was to have the owner move it.

Once the cash passed through the tedious customs and immigration check at the destination, it was a simple job to relieve the owner of the currency. He and Enzo had perfected the process over many years and many chumps.

Luigi smiled. He saw the Grantlys ahead of him. They were in a different line, talking to a security guard. The guard pointed to some piece of paper. No doubt, they were asking for directions. Old people were always asking for directions.

He passed through security. The Grantlys were repacking the contents of the hand luggage. They would be through in a few moments. He breathed a sigh of relief, and walked off to find a decent espresso before the flight.

Luigi felt confident extra dollars would reach his Swiss bank account by Thursday. He could take the weekend off. Spend time with Lenora. Or Maria. Or Sophie. Maybe one each day. Why not?

Everything was going to work out. The Grantlys would arrive in New York, then fly to Rome with the final payment.

When they reached Rome, the money would change hands. Depending on how they acted, they would be allowed to return with Wilson, or they would not.

Luigi was already leaning toward not.

# CHAPTER TWENTY-FIVE

*Orlando, Florida*
*May 11*

JESS FOUND A PHARMACY, and bought antiseptic wipes and a handful of toiletries. In the restroom, she daubed the antiseptic over the cuts and scrapes on her arm. Her arms and legs ached, partly from her exertions, and partly from the stress that had been burning in her muscles. She cleaned her face, did the best she could with her hair, and applied a little make up.

Unlike dozens of the crash victims she'd seen on one of the airport televisions, she was good to go.

Feeling slightly more human, she toured the airport shops, grabbing a few days' worth of clothes. She picked out a brown canvas duffle bag for luggage. She hid the Glock inside a thick padding of her new clothes, packed it in the middle of the duffel, and filled the rest of the space with new toiletries and more clothing.

She returned to the pharmacy, purchased a pay-as-you-go cell phone, and activated it. Just in case.

She searched out the Skyway Airlines check-in desk, and claimed her tickets using an automated kiosk. She ignored an expectant check-in guy, took the steps down to the arrival road, and dropped the bag with a porter at the curbside check-in counter, as Morris had instructed. The man checked her ticket and ID twice before handing it back to her.

"This it?" he said, hefting her bag from the scales.

"That's all," she said.

He raised his eyebrows, and proceeded to toss the bag on the conveyer. She watched it disappear through a thick plastic curtain, and immediately regretted not having searched a little longer for a hard-sided case.

She walked back into the terminal. At least Morris had her covered. The gun should pass through screening and make it to New York. Always assuming someone didn't steal it before she collected it. Not a great plan, but since her airline-approved hard case with the lock only she could open was still in the back of the burnt-out rental at the bottom of a ditch, it was the best she could do. She bit her lip. Nothing to be done about the gun now. If it didn't arrive in New York City, she'd deal with that problem when she came to it. She'd have to do better if she was forced to take the flight to Rome.

Jess stood in line through security and arrived at her gate early. She brought up the photo she had taken in the Grantlys' house to familiarize herself with their appearance. She wandered around the gate and the nearby shops, but there was no sign of them.

She bought a gossip rag in one of the shops, and stood against a wall that afforded a good view of the boarding area.

People changed seats at the counter and the clerk updated the time until boarding. A couple in leathers and nose piercings had an argument. But the Grantlys were nowhere to be seen.

She pulled her ticket from her messenger bag and checked the departure time. The board behind the desk showed the same time. She glanced at her watch. Twenty minutes. Where the hell were they?

A 737 arrived, easing to a halt just feet from the jet bridge. The clerk vacated the counter and carded her way through the security door to the aircraft. A few moments later, the jet bridge shook as it covered the last few feet to touch the skin of the 737.

The passengers deplaned. They shuffled out of the security door, stretching and yawning as they struggled with oversized carry-on bags.

The sign behind the counter still listed departure as on time. The same sign listed the scheduled flight time as two hours and forty minutes, non-stop Orlando to JFK.

The gate agents set up for boarding. They called for families traveling with children, and anyone else needing a little extra time for boarding, and the usual rush of people crowded the jet bridge entrance. A single mother with two toddlers waved her arms and tried to push through, only to give up halfway to the door.

There was no sign of the Grantlys. Jess looked up and down the length of the terminal corridor. Numbers hung from plaques on the ceiling, denoting each gate. Large signs. Clear numbers. White digits on a dark blue background. Surely, they couldn't be lost?

The gate agent invited first class passengers to board.

Jess checked her ticket. First class. An aisle seat. She had the tickets for the two seats across the aisle as well. Space for the Grantlys. They would be seated a few rows behind her in coach. Mid-cabin, perhaps? Small seats. Cramped. Tough for a ninety year old. But once they were airborne, she'd move them to first class. A little comfort. Room to stretch out. Better food. Some wine, maybe. Anything to get them to open up. To get them to talk. To reveal whatever they might know of their son and his captors. Anything to get them out of the affair alive.

Jess flipped the pages of the gossip magazine, and listened for Roger's radio-announcer voice. She'd never forget it. But she didn't hear him now.

The gate agent began seating coach class.

The last passengers vacated their terminal seats, and lined up at the jet bridge, tickets in hand.

Jess bit her lip. The Grantlys should be in that same line. They couldn't miss the flight. Not after they left home so early.

Jess's skin tingled. Left home early? What if that meant they'd changed their plans? Taken a different route for a different plan? A typical hostage trick. Without the Grantlys, she had no way to track down their son, Wilson, and the scammers. They get what they could from the Grantlys, and carry on. New victims, new money, new torment. All because she'd lost the parents.

Jess swore. Where the hell were they?

# CHAPTER TWENTY-SIX

*Orlando, Florida*
*May 11*

JESS STUFFED HER MAGAZINE in her bag, and moved away from the boarding area. Without the Grantlys, there was no purpose to her traveling to New York. She pulled out her phone. Morris needed to know.

The gate attendant picked up a microphone. "Last call for Flight 1804 to JFK. Now boarding. Flight 1804. If you have confirmed seats on this flight, you must board now."

Jess turned her phone over in her hand. The Grantlys' car company. She shouldn't have left it to Miss Fuchsia to check on them. If she'd done it herself she would have confirmed the destination.

The last of the passengers disappeared down the jet bridge.

The gate attendant's voice rang out. "Passengers Kimball, Grantly and Grantly, last call for New York. Last call for Kimball, Grantly and Grantly."

More names were called, but she'd tuned out. Jess ran her

thumb over her phone's keyboard. What was she going to tell Morris?

Roger Grantly's radio voice wafted through the air. "Come on, Harriet. I can't believe you brought knitting needles in your bag. What were you thinking? They're going to leave us here. Get a move on."

Jess smiled, stuffed her phone in her bag, and rummaged for her ticket.

Harriet hustled after her husband. "I'm coming. I only wanted to work on my baby bonnets. What's wrong with that? Besides, they didn't confiscate them."

Roger waved his hand. "But they almost made us miss our flight."

If the situation weren't so heartbreaking, Jess would have laughed out loud. She stole a glance at them in line. Roger was wearing a beige seersucker suit that he'd probably bought during the Carter administration. His right hand held Harriet's elbow firmly, hurrying her along. In his left hand, he held their boarding passes and the head of a cane. An ancient, but still dapper, Panama rested comfortably atop his head. His face was red and sweating.

Harriet wore a lime green floral church dress, white gloves, and sensible pumps. Her pink lipstick was askew, but her blue eyes twinkled behind thick lenses that magnified excited pupils.

Jess guessed the woman had probably never flown before. Her obvious excitement and apprehension mixed with her bewilderment that anyone could object to the knitting of infant caps endeared the woman to her. When they met, Jess would tell her so.

Jess gave them a moment to enter the jet bridge, and hurried to the gate, her ticket held out. The gate attendant scowled as she swiped the boarding pass under the scanner. Jess followed the couple onto the aircraft, staying back several paces so they wouldn't be suspicious when she talked to them later. She slipped into her first class seat under the glower of her fellow travelers.

# CHAPTER TWENTY-SEVEN

*Orlando, Florida*
*May 11*

LUIGI PURCHASED A NEWSPAPER at a terminal stand, tucked it under his arm, and watched the activity around the gate for New York. The usual boarding rituals had been attended to, but the Grantlys had not arrived. The boarding line was down to its last few passengers.

An attractive American woman leaned against the far wall. Their eyes met briefly. Her blonde hair curled around her face in a fetching way. Slightly darker golden eyebrows arched above softly tinted eyelids. She looked full of nervous energy, shifting her weight from foot to foot. He debated speaking to her. He wanted to hear her voice. Was it musical? Husky? He imagined her whispering intimately into his ear across a silk pillow.

She looked as if she might be boarding the New York flight, but as the line shortened, she moved away from the gate.

Still there was no sign of the Grantlys. He cursed himself

for having left them. It still wasn't inconceivable they had changed their minds. They would have some explaining to do, but the American authorities might allow them to leave the airport after check-in and even though they'd checked luggage.

Damn. He ground his teeth. The tedium had worn him down, and he'd fallen into its trap. He'd been sloppy. He imagined Enzo's rage if he screwed up this simple task after having come so close to success.

Just as he swore to himself a dozen times for becoming complacent and sloppy, he saw the Grantlys coming down the corridor. They seemed to be arguing, at least as much as two ninety-year-olds could argue. Not like Italians argued, with gusto and passion. Not even close.

Luigi watched as they held out their boarding passes to the gate agent, and boarded the plane.

He stepped out of the newsstand and crossed the corridor toward the gate. The American woman stuffed her phone in a large bag, waved a boarding pass at the gate attendant, and followed the Grantlys down the jet bridge.

Luigi faked a frantic, last-minute search through his pockets to give them time and distance. The last thing he wanted was to be recognized. The gate agent scowled. After a few moments, he produced his boarding pass. The gate agent slapped it under the scanner, waited for the beep, and shoved it back in his hand.

"We need on-time boarding for an on-time departure," she scolded exactly like his mother used to do when he misbehaved as a boy, rest her soul.

Luigi nodded as if he cared before he strolled down the jet bridge making sure to stay far enough behind the Grantlys.

Inside the cabin, he cussed at the sight of two empty first

class seats when he'd been told the cabin was full.

Across the aisle from the empty seats, the American woman fussed with her phone. He guessed she had stayed around the gate until the last minute waiting for a call from her boyfriend. He held back a sneer. Americans couldn't live without constant communication and she was nothing more than another needy woman, clinging to a man who had better things to do. He crossed her off his mental list. He was all too familiar with that type. He'd accumulated too many women exactly like that already.

In the middle of the coach section, one of the stewards helped the Grantlys load their overstuffed carry-ons into the overhead bins. He strained to close the door then gestured for the old couple to sit. Harriet thanked him profusely, to the point of embarrassment before she wiggled herself into the middle seat. Roger plopped down heavily into the aisle seat, leaned his head back, and closed his eyes.

Harriet settled back, too, with a smile on her face, and a paperback with a half-naked cowboy on the cover in her hand. Roger fought to close the seatbelt over his protruding stomach, breathing heavily.

Luigi continued to his seat, three rows behind the Grantlys on the opposite side of the aircraft. He had a good view of the couple. No one questioned a man staring forward in an aircraft, so he could observe them for every moment of the flight without suspicion. Perhaps, for the first leg of the long journey to Rome, watching them was the better move. They still had a layover and plane change in New York. There were plenty of opportunities for them to screw things up, or change their minds.

He stretched his back. Yes, he would make the most of his clear view of the Grantlys now, and fly in the first class cabin on the longer trip to Rome tonight.

The steward handed him a complimentary headset. Luigi stuffed the filthy earphones into the seat pocket, and opened his newspaper.

He heard Harriet and Roger still arguing over the embarrassing scene with her knitting needles at the security checkpoint. They were such fools. He'd be glad to be rid of them. The sooner the better.

Harriet, the one he'd had the most contact with the past few days, chattered incessantly. This was a trait her son had concealed when they communicated by e-mail. Now, he realized it was a problem, and would slow them down considerably because he'd be required to deal with her, instead of ignoring her as he'd otherwise have done.

He'd need to adjust his plans. He couldn't rush her. She had to feel safe and comfortable until they were safely buckled in on Flight 12 tonight. Because once they were in the air, enroute to Rome, there would be no turning back.

Luigi turned the page of his newspaper. He and Enzo ran a business based entirely on selling, and the psychology of selling was based solely on trust. If Harriet didn't like and trust him, she would be a constant problem. He'd taken innumerable sales courses over the years and trust was the one absolute. But sometimes, with a pigeon like Harriet, the sales process was a challenge beyond his patience.

Harriet had kept up her chatter. Roger said almost nothing. The old goat looked red. He fanned himself with the in-flight magazine, and mopped his brow with a cotton handkerchief. As the steward checked seatbelts for takeoff, he handed the old man a bottle of water. Roger Grantly took a long draught, and leaned back on the headrest again.

Luigi curled his lip. Don't stroke out, old man. Not before we conclude our business tomorrow. After that, I'll be happy to kill you myself and put both of us out of our misery.

# CHAPTER TWENTY-EIGHT

*Orlando, Florida*
*May 11*

THE FLIGHT ATTENDANT CLOSED the bulkhead door. The jet bridge retracted. A small tractor pushed the plane back from the gate.

When she felt the plane move, Jess relaxed for the first time in twenty-four hours. The Grantlys would be captive until they reached New York. No harm could possibly come to them. So far, so good.

She pulled earphones out of her bag, closed her eyes and took a sorely needed power nap.

When she awakened refreshed, the plane had reached cruising altitude, and the attendants were in the cabin with the beverage cart.

"Drink?" said the flight attendant.

"Coffee, black, please."

He poured the coffee, and she took the cup. "Since we have two empty seats here, would you mind inviting my friends

Mr. and Mrs. Grantly to join us?"

"Er...I don't think we're supposed—"

Jess placed a hand on his forearm. "They're both in their nineties and he's not feeling well. You could act like it was your idea. Or airline policy or something." She raised her eyebrows. "Would you mind?"

He seemed to think it over for a moment and shrugged. "Sure. Why not? I'll be right back."

He returned several minutes later with the Grantlys waddling along the narrow aisle behind him. He gestured to the empty seats. "Here you are. This will give you a more comfortable seat and some breathing room during the flight. But we'll need to return you to your assigned seats for landing, okay?"

Harriet placed her hand on the big leather seat. "Oh my, yes! Why this is lovely! Look at all the room, Roger!" She scooted awkwardly into the window seat, and became immediately engrossed by the clouds.

Roger said nothing. He grunted as he plopped down in the aisle seat directly across from Jess. He used a soggy handkerchief to mop his head and neck. He closed his eyes, and leaned his head back against the headrest. His breathing was labored and irregular.

Jess gave him a few moments to recover from his exertion, leaned across the aisle, and tapped his arm. "Mr. Grantly?"

He didn't respond. At first, she thought he'd passed out, but then he opened his eyes and looked at her.

She cleared her throat. "Mr. Grantly, my name is Jessica Kimball. I stopped by your son's office this morning to speak with him, and your receptionist sent me to your home."

He frowned, confused. "What? You were at my home?"

Jess kept her voice as gentle as possible, given the white

noise of the aircraft. "But you'd already left for the airport, so I came here."

"Here? On this flight?" He frowned and glared at her.

"You're following me?"

"Not exactly. I'm here to help."

"With what?"

"With your son."

He sat up straighter, and wiped his face with the soggy handkerchief. "What do you know about my son?"

"More than you might think, but I don't know enough. We've got almost two hours for you to fill me in."

"About what?"

"I'm working with the FBI. We want to help you get your son back alive."

He inched away from her. The sweat that had dappled his forehead, now dripped down into his eyes. He swiped with the handkerchief again.

Jess stood and adjusted the air vent above his head, directing as much cold air onto his face as she could. He stared straight ahead. Not looking at her or acknowledging her actions.

Harriet twittered on about the clouds and the plane and the patchwork of land she saw from time to time on the ground.

Roger continued to sweat profusely even though the air-conditioning blasting from the plane's overhead air vents was enough to refrigerate ice cream.

Jess struggled to keep impatience from showing on her face as she waited for him to comprehend his situation and accept her help.

Finally he levered himself from his seat with his cane. "Harriet. Let's go."

Harriet tore her gaze away from the view, and watched him.

He swayed and grabbed the seat in front. The plane shook. Minor clear air turbulence. Nothing more. He shifted his balance and moved the cane to compensate, but his jerky movements were too slow, and he thumped back into his seat.

Jess reached over and placed a comforting hand on his arm. "Mr. Grantly, I want to help you save your son's life. You and Harriet can't possibly do this on your own."

His shoulders slumped. He closed his eyes, and his head sagged back on the headrest. The flight attendant returned with the beverage service. He served Roger a bottle of water and Harriet an iced tea, and moved on to the next set of passengers.

Roger opened his eyes and took a sip of the water. "Tell me what you think you know, Ms. Kimball. And then we'll see if there's anything you can do for my son." His resigned tone seemed like a step forward.

Harriet looked at Jess through thick glasses that made her blue eyes look like saucers.

Jess took a deep breath. "I believe your son has been the victim of sophisticated thieves." A half-truth, but the best opening she could come up with.

Roger nodded almost imperceptibly. He needed to be pushed in the right direction.

"He's probably been taking money from Grantly and Son to pay the thieves, which is why you don't want to get the FBI involved." She took a deep breath. "But we suspect he's been kidnapped, and that you're on your way to Rome to pay the ransom to get him back."

Harriet gasped.

"And," Jess dragged out the word, "I know for sure that you're never going to make it to Rome, let alone bring your son home, unless you let me help you."

"How can you possibly know that?" Harriet's indignation was as heartbreaking as the entire situation. If Wilson Grantly had been sitting within twenty feet of her, Jess would have cheerfully tackled him and pummeled him within an inch of his life. What was he thinking, putting his parents in this situation?

Jess's gaze met Harriet's directly and didn't flinch. "Because the FBI is watching you, and if you don't take me up on my offer, the FBI will arrest you before you get on that plane tonight."

Harriet's entire body was rigid. Color rose in her cheeks. "Arrest us? For what?"

"It doesn't matter, does it?" Jess leaned in. "Aiding and abetting your son's crimes? Whatever it is, if you're arrested, you won't be in Rome tomorrow, and that's the end, isn't it?"

Harriet's lips formed a perfect circle. She leaned back and clutched her pearls. She said, "Oh," in a whispery voice that Jess could barely hear.

"Five of your son's friends are already dead or missing or in prison. At this point, prison would be the safest place for Wilson." Jess cocked her head and frowned. "Otherwise..."

At that, Harriet began to cry. Which was the last straw for Roger. He seemed to deflate before Jess's very eyes. He slumped in his seat, and patted Harriet's hand.

When he spoke again, Jess heard weary resignation in his tone. "What is it you want to know?"

"Let's start with exactly where and when you are supposed to deliver the ransom."

"Tomorrow. They're meeting us at the airport. In Rome." Roger made strong eye contact and flashed a curt nod. "We give them the money, they give us Wilson. We have a return flight booked three hours later."

Jess nodded. A simple plan. Appealing. Easy. The sort of thing that sounded sensible to sensible people. People brought up with a clear view of what was right, and what was not. She bit her lip. People from the twenties. Not the world they lived in today.

The roaring twenties were a long time ago. Things had changed. The world wasn't so clear-cut anymore, even if it had been then. The plan wouldn't be simple. There wouldn't be a handshake and a smile and a pat on the back. Money exchanged. Wilson freed. Problem over. Come home.

Jess had written extensively about kidnappings. She'd been living her own nightmare with her son, Peter's kidnapping for ten long years. These things were never so simple. Ever.

She took a deep breath. "How will you get the money?"

Roger frowned. "Get it? What's to get?"

"The...don't tell me you have the ransom money with you?"

"Of course."

"Not a money order, or a bearer bond, or, or...anything?"

"Absolutely not." Roger's chin dipped another curt nod, as if her suggestion was preposterous.

The situation was spiraling downward with every new piece of INTEL she managed to acquire. She cleared her throat. "How much cash are we talking about?"

Roger lowered his voice. "Two hundred and thirty-seven thousand dollars." He gazed straight into Jess's eyes. "Everything we have left." His words were slow. Individual. Painful.

Jess looked at Roger then Harriet. She had no clue how much nearly a quarter million dollars would weigh, but neither of them could possibly be carrying that much cash on their bodies. And the security search should have found it in their carry-on bags because U.S. currency contained metal strips that were visible on baggage x-ray machines.

She felt a sinking sensation in her stomach. "You packed it into your checked luggage?"

Roger gave another single, slow and sure nod. "We couldn't carry it."

Jess weighed her words carefully. She didn't want to scare them more than necessary. But they had to know they'd increase their activities to the felony level for sure if they transported that cash to Rome. "You know, the banks are required to report large withdrawals to the government. So, if you—"

Harriet lifted her chest, and tossed her shoulders back. "We didn't withdraw the money from the bank. We're old, dear, but we're not stupid."

Jess breathed a few times before she said, "Where did you get it, then?"

Harriet's blue-eyed gaze was tinged with a touch of steel. "We keep cash around. Always have. Banks can't always be trusted, dear."

Jess exhaled. "Would Wilson know you had that money in the house?"

"Of course. We wanted him to know where it was in case anything happened to us." Her eyes twinkled now. She patted Jess's hand. "Our friend, Sally Mitchell? She stashed money in books and in the freezer and all over her house. When she died, it took her kids two years to find it all. And they were never sure they'd located all her hiding places. They couldn't even sell the house for the longest time because they were so worried about whether they'd found all the money."

It was all Jess could do not to swear. Wilson must have told the kidnappers about the hidden cash, the people he had involved himself with in the first place, and dragged his parents into the extortion.

She didn't quite know what to say. The flight attendant walked down the aisle, interrupting the conversation for a moment. Jess rested her head on the back of her seat and closed her eyes.

Jess had been inside their home. She imagined how they'd done this crazy thing. Roger must have looked at Harriet for agreement. She'd nodded. They said nothing because everything that could be said, had been said.

They felt they'd had no choice.

They'd have levered themselves from the chairs, and collected their life savings together. The money was probably spread around their house. Hidden under floorboards, behind cupboards, and inside false-bottomed boxes in their pantry. The dollars they had accumulated through long hard years of honest work, and the pennies they had saved, eating in, drinking water with their meals, forgoing cable TV for the free signals that came snowy over the air.

They'd have sorted the money on their dining room table. The hundreds next to the fifties. The twenties by the tens and lower denominations. Colorful, crisp bills. Short stacks butted against each other. The twenties, tens, and ones taking up most of the space. A thin elastic band surrounding each bundle. A post-it note recording each stack's value.

They'd added up the post-it notes. Once each. Their numbers agreeing, a miracle given their shaking hands and failing eyesight. They recorded their numbers on a sheet of paper, and memorized the total before tucking it behind the supplies in the pantry. Hiding the evidence. Not from the neighbors or the police, but from themselves.

They'd wrapped the bundles in plastic grocery bags, and secured them with short strips of cellophane tape. They'd paused a moment to look at the sight on their kitchen table. The tight plastic pressing on the corners of the thick wedges of bills. The grocery store emblems twisted between the folds that sealed the packages. Plastic folded over plastic. Waterproofed as best as they could manage.

"Better safe than sorry," Mrs. Grantly probably said.

Mr. Grantly's lip had trembled. His knees quivered. He'd sat down. A chair beside the table. "Everything we have in the world."

She'd taken the chair beside him, their knees touching. He'd put his hand on hers. She'd wrapped a thumb over the back of his hand. Tears came. Sniffles. Gasps. Tight grips of bony knuckles. Salty drops trickling down faces. A prelude to sobs, to hugs, to tissues.

To brave words.

They'd bolstered each other's reserves, raised their morale, and stiffened their resolve. They were doing the right thing. The only thing. The only thing they could do for their only son.

They'd carried the bags, pausing a moment outside the door to their son's room to remember happier times.

They packed the money in an old blue suitcase, a layer of clothes all the way round. Protection from the elements and prying eyes alike. They placed the suitcase in the far corner of their bedroom, as if the distance dulled the pain of what they were doing. What they had to do. For Wilson.

They had no choice. That much Jess clearly understood.

The flight attendant passed through the cabin and they were free to talk across the aisle again.

Jess said, "You know that moving that much cash out of the

country is illegal? If you get caught, you'll both go to prison."

Roger put his palms together as if he was praying and leaned the fingers against his chin. "Do you have children, Ms. Kimball?"

It was an everyday question. Normal enough. A conversation starter usually. But for Jess the question was always a warning. A red flag signaling danger to come. The conversation moving into areas she could not and would not attempt to discuss.

She took a deep breath for strength and offered the answer she always gave. Not a lie, but not the full truth, either. "No, I don't."

Roger nodded as if he'd expected as much. "Our youngest son died. Iraq. Eight years ago. In combat. Second Infantry division." He pushed his lower lip out then brought it back in, his feelings not weakened, but harnessed. He looked at Jess, his face much ruddier than it should have been. "If you had only one son left, you would do anything to keep him alive. You'd pay anything. Go anywhere. Do whatever you had to do." His face was an even brighter crimson now. His chest rose and fell as if he were on the verge of tears he refused to shed. "Wilson asked. Our son wanted help from us. So how could we not help him?"

"But there are many ways to help—"

He shook his head. "We already sacrificed one son for our country, Ms Kimball." He breathed noisily through his nose. "Tell me you wouldn't do exactly what we are doing."

Jess sighed. She couldn't voice the lie. Of course, she would be doing exactly what they had done. She'd done much harder things for Peter. She'd do them again. And she wouldn't care whether some lawyer said she'd committed a crime or not.

She glanced at her watch. Less than an hour of flight time left before they landed in New York. She'd have to call Morris, and he would have to bring in an FBI team. She was way out of her element, and the Grantlys were even further afield. No matter how much they wanted to help their son, there was little chance Roger and Harriet would survive their crazy scheme, let alone Wilson Grantly, who might even be dead already.

Harriet leaned past Roger and whispered, "Do you really think we'll be stopped? From saving our son?"

Jess swallowed. Wilson was a heartless, sniveling coward to sell his parents out in such a scam, but she understood their blind love for the son, and the pain their failure would bring. "We'll find a way, or..." She couldn't promise anything from Morris. He'd already made that clear. "*I* will find a way."

She leaned back in her seat and closed her eyes. Kidnappers, a hostage, two feeble but determined ninety-year-olds, and a quarter million dollars. She had no idea how to fix any of that, but she was working on it.

# CHAPTER TWENTY-NINE

LUIGI GLANCED AT HIS watch. They'd been flying for almost two hours. The plane was on schedule. They would be landing in New York shortly.

After takeoff, the Grantlys had been moved into the first class cabin. He couldn't see them on the other side of the privacy curtain, but he wasn't worried. Where could they go at thirty-thousand feet? He'd find them easily enough when the plane landed.

The flight attendant announced the captain had begun the initial descent, and instructed passengers to return to their seats. Harriet pushed aside the first class cabin curtain, and preceded Roger to row eighteen. She reclaimed her center seat, and Roger sunk heavily into the seat on the aisle.

The seat back monitor in front of Luigi indicated the plane would land at John F. Kennedy International Airport in twenty minutes. He closed his eyes for a brief period of quiet before he'd be subjected to Harriet's incessant babbling again.

The next time he looked, Roger's head had fallen to one side. The old man was sleeping. Luigi's father had slept a lot in his final years. But then, his father hadn't been well. When he'd died of a massive heart attack, Luigi had been with him through his last hours. He'd had nausea and sickness, trouble breathing, pains in his side and arm. He remembered the pain in his father's chest had grown unbearable. Luigi had left to bring him a glass of water, but when he returned, his father's head had lolled over, much as Roger's did now.

Luigi sat up straight. Was the old guy having a heart attack? He'd certainly been sweating and red in the face. If Roger died, the deal could die with him. Luigi hadn't come this far to see the deal fall apart now.

He looked up and down the length of the aircraft. The flight attendants were busy preparing for landing. He needed to do something to keep Roger alive. But what? Without bringing attention to himself? Precious seconds lumbered past.

Luigi stood and walked toward the front of the plane. When he reached Roger's seat, he swung his hip and bumped Roger's shoulder, hard, pushing the old man's head onto Harriet's shoulder. She turned, probably to scold her husband or start another stream of her babbling nonsense, but instead, began to scream. Thank God.

Luigi walked on to the first class cabin, stepping aside as the flight attendants rushed toward Harriet's screams. He ducked into the restroom, and sat on the toilet lid to wait. There was a request on the intercom for a doctor.

After a few minutes, Luigi emerged and headed toward his seat. Old man Grantly had been moved to the rear of the plane, Harriet beside him. The old guy was moving a bit, which was a good sign.

"What happened?" Luigi asked a young mother seated by the window, holding her baby to her chest.

"That old man. Back there. They think he had a heart attack. It's just awful!" she said, tears threatening her pretty, green eyes.

"Yes, it is," Luigi agreed. And it was. Because if he didn't do something quickly to get the Grantlys back on track, his carefully constructed plan would fall apart, and with it, his quarter million dollars. To say nothing of his brother. Luigi shuddered. He'd felt the brunt of Enzo's fury before. An experience he'd move heaven and earth to avoid.

# CHAPTER THIRTY

*New York City, New York*
*May 11*

WHEN THE PLANE LANDED, the day was sunny and mild. The captain asked all passengers to remain in their seats while the patient was removed to the waiting ambulance. Jess watched the paramedics lift Roger from the aircraft's rear exit. They escorted Harriet down the exterior air stairs.

Roger looked older and frailer than ever. His red face had turned pale. Harriet's bubbly energy had evaporated. Gone were the bright blue eyes that sparkled with mischief. The pair looked every moment of their ages.

Jess felt her anger building. Wilson Grantly had involved himself in a dirty money scheme and then roped his parents into it as well. They were ninety years old, and he was treating them as he must have all his life. As a convenience, a useful source of money, someone to sacrifice for his own hide. Jess could muster no sympathy for Wilson Grantly. He and Blazek were two of a kind.

Harriet stood alone on the tarmac, her needleless bag of yarn by her side. Roger was being loaded into the ambulance. Jess clenched her fists. She couldn't do it. She couldn't let them make any more sacrifices. She grabbed her bag, rushed to the back of the aircraft, and down the stairs to the tarmac.

She reached Harriet while they were still securing Roger into the ambulance. "Mrs. Grantly?" Jess said, gently touching her arm to avoid startling her.

Harriet turned around. Her eyes didn't focus on Jess. "Yes, dear?"

"Harriet, let me help you."

"Oh, my dear, I'm quite sure you cannot help me. Although I wish you could," Harriet said.

Roger was secured in the ambulance, motionless, breathing through an oxygen mask. The paramedic turned his attention to Harriet. "It's time to go Mrs. Grantly," he said, offering her a hand to climb into the back with Roger.

Harriet looked around. She stepped behind Jess, scanning the tarmac. "Where is our luggage? I need our bags. They, they…" She grabbed Jess's arm. "We need them."

Jess patted her hand. "I know."

Harriet looked at the ambulance, and the paramedic with his hand outstretched. She swallowed. A tear ran down her cheek. She wiped her nose and pressed her lips together, but her chin still quivered.

Jess wrapped her fingers through hers. "Give me your claim ticket, and let me collect your luggage. You can go with Roger. I'll find you. We'll get this all worked out."

Harriet held her fist over her mouth. "I…I…"

"We have to go, lady," called the paramedic.

Jess turned to the paramedic. "What's your name?"

"Callum Black."

"I'm Jessica Kimball. Thanks for taking good care of my friends. Where are you taking him?"

"We're required to transport him to the closest facility, Antigua Hospital," Callum Black said. "Mrs. Grantly? We need to go. Now."

Harriet's chin still quivered and she pressed her fist to her mouth to silence her sobs. Jess gave her a hug. "You're tired and overwhelmed right now, Harriet. You go with Roger. I'll collect your luggage and meet you at the hospital. It will be all right."

Harriet used a handkerchief to wipe her tears. "I'm so worried."

"I'm a good worrier. I've had tons of practice." Jess squeezed her shoulder gently. "You take care of Roger and let me worry for a while, okay?"

Jess pulled out two of her business cards. She gave one to Harriet, along with the burner cell phone she had purchased at the Orlando airport. Harriet stared at the phone. "I don't know how to use one of these," Harriet said, voice unsteady.

Jess patted her arm. "When I have your luggage, I will call you. All you have to do is press this green button and then talk to me." She pointed to the button. "You can do that, can't you?"

"I think so." Harriet opened her handbag and removed the ticket envelope containing her baggage claim checks. "Please be very careful, Jess. You know how important this…the luggage, and everything, is to us."

"It will all be fine." Jess accepted the envelope, nodded and squeezed Harriet's shoulder one last time. "I'll see you very soon."

The paramedic helped Harriet into the ambulance.

Jess waited for him to close the door. She handed another

business card to Callum Black in exchange for his. "Is Antigua a heart center?"

He shook his head. "It's a trauma center. They might transfer him if he needs cardiac care beyond their staff."

"Is it possible he'll be examined and released?"

The paramedic shook his head. "I'm no doctor and I can't discuss his medical care with you, but it looks like he had a heart attack, and his wife said he's had them before. So, somebody's gonna want to keep him overnight. Observation at the very least." He shrugged. "Liability being what it is these days."

"I'll call you," Jess said.

"You do that." The words didn't seem reassuring, but his demeanor did.

Jess watched the ambulance drive away, lights flashing. She climbed back up the steps, and retook her seat.

A bad heart. A known condition. A stressful day. Not a good combination. Now they were caught between saving Roger or saving Wilson. Jess had no doubt which one was more worth saving, but without Wilson, she couldn't save Roger, either. Losing his only son would surely kill him.

Stress caused his heart attack. No surprise. Unless Jess could stop him, the thief would escape with the money Wilson had already paid him. All three Grantlys would go to jail and all three lives would be effectively over. How many would these thieves kill before they were stopped? Nothing Jess could do about that. But she could do her best to see that Harriet and Roger were not two of their murder victims.

Once Jess was on board, the rear aircraft door closed, and the plane finished taxiing to the terminal. She lined up with the rest of the passengers, and exited the cabin. Those continuing to connecting flights dodged and weaved their way through the throng to reach their gates before boarding ended.

She didn't have that problem. The Rome flight didn't depart until midnight. She'd bought the ticket as insurance, but she knew now she was going to use it. That's where the scammer was. That's where he was waiting for Harriet and Roger. And their money.

She didn't intend to keep him waiting.

# CHAPTER THIRTY-ONE

*New York City, New York*
*May 11*

LUIGI FOLLOWED THE LINE of passengers from the plane, out into the concourse, and through security. He took the escalator down and turned left into a large hall marked "Lockers."

The hall was divided into sections, a large colored circle denoting each row. He found the blue section, and waited until a man in a business suit departed before opening the locker he'd rented several days ago.

He pulled out the untraceable .22-caliber Smith & Wesson 22A pistol. His thumb felt the rough area on the side where the serial number had once been. He took its box of ammunition, and a box cutter, and raced to baggage claim.

Old man Grantly had been taken away in the ambulance, his wife with him. That left their luggage waiting to be claimed. If they'd had any sense, they would have told the authorities about their luggage and someone official would have collected the bags.

But they had a second problem. The bags contained what was left of their life savings. Nearly a quarter million dollars. The last thing they wanted was for that money to fall into official hands.

The old man was a known quantity. He wasn't going to bounce back from a heart attack. Even if he did, the airline would deny him passage. Too much risk. Too much liability. Roger Grantly was grounded.

His wife was different. She was the more active of the two. Maybe too active. She was certainly a wild card. Luigi couldn't depend on her to carry through. She could quite likely call the whole thing off.

He wouldn't let that happen.

He had to deal with the Grantlys and retrieve the money. No excuses.

Dealing with the Grantlys wouldn't be too difficult. He would call around the area hospitals, locate, and terminate them. She was old and slow and much smaller than Luigi. No contest there. The old man would probably die in the hospital anyway. He certainly looked near death when they carried him off the plane. Old man Grantly could be dead already.

The thought cheered Luigi and made him smile. Now that the cash was in play, he'd find another way to move the money to Rome. Enzo wouldn't like it. An unnecessary risk, he'd say. Enzo was older and, he thought, wiser than Luigi. But Luigi was the better improviser. He'd figure out what to do, if things went sideways.

The money was always his first priority. The three Grantlys were nothing but annoying details.

He worked his way along the row of conveyor belts until he found his flight number. He recognized several of his fellow passengers' faces crowded around the ramp where the cases emerged from deep in the airport's baggage handling system.

The attractive and meddlesome American woman was there, one hand on a luggage trolley, the other typing furiously on her phone. She had been on the tarmac, talking to Harriet when they carted the old man away.

Luigi stood on the opposite side of the conveyor, so he could casually stare in her direction. She kept her shoulders back, and he guessed she ran or worked out to keep her figure. It was a good figure. Natural muscle tone, not the Botox and silicone enhanced image of beauty pushed by Hollywood. She still seemed full of nervous energy, but the curls in her hair looked as if they'd suffered through a long day. He watched for several minutes before he realized she reminded him of an American actress. What was her name? Meg Ryan. Yes. That's the one. Only younger. Early thirties, Luigi guessed, and he was good with guessing ages.

Bags finally started rolling down the ramp onto the conveyor. People crowded closer. Luigi scanned the hall, and breathed a sigh of relief. He saw no police and no officials with clipboards and a description of the Grantlys' bags.

He turned his attention to the silver baggage belt. Luggage was collected, tags were checked, and slowly the crowd in the baggage claim area thinned out.

The American woman remained on the far side of the carousel, watching the bags pass. After a few minutes, she selected a brown duffel bag. Luigi was sure the duffel had traveled the belt's complete circuit at least a couple of times.

He kept his eyes on the conveyor. Was she ever going to leave? Did she have more bags? She settled the duffel by her feet. Damn, was she going to collect the Grantlys' luggage? Was she some part of the family that the spineless Wilson Grantly had neglected to mention? He made a note to bring it up with the man. Painfully.

The American kept her eyes on the conveyor.

Luigi recognized the Grantlys' luggage instantly when it finally appeared. Two old-fashioned hard-sided blue bags. They tumbled sideways down the ramp, and thumped against the bracing around the conveyor.

The American didn't move. She kept her eyes on the conveyor. The blue bags passed her. Perhaps she wasn't waiting for the Grantlys' bags after all? Or perhaps she didn't know what they looked like? The old woman probably couldn't remember the color, let alone the make.

The bags passed by Luigi. He fought back the temptation to grab them and run. A quarter million dollars. He could be out of the exit before anyone moved. Even if they did, he had his gun. An easy and effective deterrent to the average do-gooder. He wouldn't even need to fire.

But he had to be patient. He had to be sure there was no surveillance. Not the American, not airport officials, nor the New York police. A few minutes would flush out any suspects. The general lack of interest in the Grantlys' bags would bring them out. As much as he hated the idea of losing the money, he hated the idea of losing his liberty even more.

The bags passed by again. One more circuit.

He looked around the claim area. Near the exit was a men's restroom. He could use it to remove the ransom. After, he would stow the cash in his locker, and jam the bags into another. He couldn't leave the bags in the open. If they were discovered, it wouldn't take long for them to be connected to the Grantlys, and that would invite more problems.

He took a deep breath. The bags turned the corner of the

conveyor again. One more leg, along the far side, and they would be his.

The American was still waiting. He laughed to himself. Her luggage was probably lost. Would she be distraught? Or would she have a screaming fit with some underpaid airline flunky? Either way, he didn't intend to be around to find out. Thirty seconds more and she'd be left waiting here alone.

He dried his hand on his jeans, ready to grip the plastic handles of the Grantlys' heavy luggage.

He took a step toward the belt.

The bags closed on the American. She stepped forward. He shivered. She took another step. He took a half step, his eyes narrowing on her. She stepped forward, both hands out, and lifted both of the Grantlys' bags from the conveyer.

The muscles in his face went rigid. He eased his hands to his sides and clenched them into fists. Damn her. Damn her to hell.

He had to stay controlled. Focused. He took a deep breath. Damn her. He watched the bags.

She checked the tags, lifted them onto her trolley, and headed for the exit.

Damn her. He forced himself to breathe until his chest rose and fell rhythmically. He stood still a few seconds, oxygenating his muscles, fighting back his temper.

He'd known all along he would have to deal with the Grantlys. But now he had to retrieve the money as well. Damn Marek. This entire fiasco was his fault. Enzo had been right.

Luigi uncoiled his fingers and breathed out his rage. The American walked through the automatic doors to the sidewalk outside. He strolled after her, following her bouncing, curly blonde hair.

Very soon, the meddlesome woman was going to die.

# CHAPTER THIRTY-TWO

*New York City, New York*
*May 11*

JESS MANEUVERED THE AIRPORT trolley through the automatic doors at the end of the baggage claim hall, and onto the sidewalk. She found her Glock in her brown duffel bag, made sure it was still covered with a layer of clothes, and moved it into her messenger bag. Whatever Morris had done to get her gun through several layers of security had obviously worked. She'd thank him next time they talked. Meanwhile, she loaded the gun along with its magazine inside the bag, and placed the clothes back in the duffel. She didn't think she needed the gun, but she wouldn't be caught without it.

She headed toward the area reserved for taxis and limousines. Several of the drivers smiled and offered to take her wherever she wanted, but she walked by them. She'd texted Mandy to arrange a limo. A company on *Taboo's* roster of approved providers. The last thing she needed was an unreliable driver while she was carrying the Grantlys' life savings and a gun not registered in New York.

A man in a black suit and a peaked cap stood beside a black Lincoln Town Car. "Kimball?" he said as she approached.

She smiled. "That's right." He put her bags in the trunk.

She slipped into the rear seat, gave him the name of the hospital, and moments later, they merged into outbound JFK traffic.

She stretched her shoulders, and rotated her head as far as it would go. Stretching her ligaments felt good. Left then right. Once. Twice. The tension in her neck eased with each rotation.

She looked to her left and caught a glimpse of the last man she'd seen at the baggage carousel. He was getting into a taxi behind her. His bags must have come out right as she'd left.

He'd been staring at her while they waited in baggage claim. He was good looking, in an unshaven, swarthy way. His jeans and blazer were worn, and his loafers scuffed. She figured him for a party-hardy kind of guy.

At a different time, it might have been interesting to meet him, but not now. She turned away, and licked her upper lip. There never seemed to be a good time for a personal life now. Would that ever change?

A sign on the Town Car's dashboard identified her driver as Omar. He was obviously familiar with the roads, navigating the lanes and orange cones smoothly.

She leaned back, and dialed Morris.

He answered on the third ring. "What news?"

"You first."

He huffed. "Wilson Grantly flew to Leonardo da Vinci airport six days ago. Confirmed. He checked into a hotel downtown."

"Is he still there?"

Morris scoffed. "Stayed two nights. Hasn't been seen since."

"Damn."

"Phone records show a call to his parents' home on the third night. Ten minutes. Three more calls after that. All from Tuscany."

"You have records?"

"Our friends at the NSA are pretty helpful these days."

"And?"

"Public payphone. Tuscany. A couple of hours north of Rome. Grows olives. It's a tourist place. Hundreds of people go through every day."

Jess sighed. "So, no clue where he's being held."

Morris said, "That's right. Unfortunately."

"Can't you do anything?"

"I'm trying to get something going with the Italians, but State is iffy."

"There's a man's life at stake."

"I know that, Jess. But what can I say? Delicate times. We can't just go into another country like we do here. There is an F in FBI. For 'federal' meaning United States, remember?"

"I remember that two ninety-year-olds were traveling halfway across the world to bring their son back, too."

"Were? What's your news?"

"Roger Grantly collapsed during the flight. Heart attack, most likely. I'm on the way to the hospital to check on him."

Morris whistled. "And his wife?"

"She went with him."

"And they're heading to Rome."

"They have tickets, but now? Who knows?"

He cleared his throat. "They confirmed he's being held for ransom?"

"Uh huh."

"You got anything more specific?"

Jess looked at Omar. He had his hands on the wheel, intently maneuvering through traffic, but he could easily hear everything she said.

She took a deep breath. "The Grantlys were told the exchange would happen at the Rome airport."

"It's not likely to be that easy. What's the ransom?"

She looked at Omar. The money was in the trunk. As nice as he appeared, the last thing she wanted to do was put temptation in front of a stranger. "I can't say."

"You don't know?"

"No. I just can't say."

"Okay. I get it. But do they have it?"

"Yes."

"Ready? In Italy?"

"It's not in Italy."

"Er..."

"Yet."

"Hell, Jess. Are you telling me they're carrying it?"

"Yes."

"If they get caught, they're looking at a butt-load of unhappiness, at the very least. Since 9/11, no government has been lenient on illegal transfers of money."

"I know."

"Is it cash? Have they been that stupid?"

"Uh-huh, and you have to understand, they lost their first child in Iraq. Wilson is all they've got. Unfortunately. He's no prize."

"You can say that again." Morris sighed. "Don't get me wrong, I'm sympathetic. But the law—"

"The law can be an ass."

"Maybe, but since the '90s, US dollars have a metal stripe. Easily visible to the TSA. It'll be stopped. They'll be stopped."

"Well, they weren't and it wasn't. But they might not be so lucky on the next flight. We have to do something."

"We're trying, Jess."

"Yeah, well—"

"And don't go getting any ideas about going to Rome."

"*Taboo* already bought the ticket."

"No, Jess. No. You've been incredibly helpful. You've turned up all this. But now—"

"I have a ticket to one of the most beautiful cities in the world. Be a shame to waste it, wouldn't you say?"

"These people aren't playing for fun. Even if this doesn't work out, we'll be better prepared the next time they start this scam," Morris said. "We'll catch them, Jess. Maybe not now, but we will."

"How can you say that? You want them to come back and—"

"You're a reporter. A civilian. And whatever happens, I don't want a bad situation made worse because you get caught up somehow. Understand?"

She blew out a long breath. "You should have seen the Grantlys."

"I know it hurts. It hurts all of us. We just have to do our best, and when that isn't good enough, we get back up, brush ourselves off, and start again."

The Town Car passed a large sign indicating Antigua Hospital. Omar took the exit.

"I'm almost at the hospital."

"Which one?"

"Antigua. They took Roger there in an ambulance from the plane. He's probably in Cardiac O.R. by now, if I had to guess."

"Okay. Just keep them talking, and I'll be there. We'll see what we can do."

"Keep them talking?"

"We flew to Newark. Preferred airline crap. Quickest I could get here. We're half an hour from you."

She breathed a sigh of relief. She wanted to help the Grantlys. She had to help them. But handing everything over to the FBI was a better idea. Morris had been more than cooperative. They both got what they expected, but there was one more thing to do before Blazek's gang could be wrapped up. And Wilson Grantly's life, his parents' last son, miserable as he was, was one big thing.

"See you soon," she said.

Before she could hang up, Morris said, "You were right about the connection between Zimmer and Blazek's extortion ring, too, Jess."

"How do you know?"

"We dug a little deeper into the Zmich and Warga murders. We found paintings by Zimmer at all three crime scenes. Thanks to you." Morris paused. "That ties all of them together and also ties them all to Blazek. If Grantly's the mastermind here, we want him, Jess."

"His parents say he's a victim of the scam, not the leader of an extortion ring, though."

"What else is a parent going to say?" Morris sighed before he hung up.

The hospital building loomed ahead. Various signs pointed to buildings and departments. Omar weaved between cars to get as close as possible to the curb at the visitor's entrance. A driver pulled out around them, gesticulating.

She leaned forward, her head between the two front seats. "You're booked all night, right?"

"All the way till midnight. Later, if you want, but you pay extra."

"Midnight's fine. Drop me by the front entrance, and wait."

Omar shook his head. "I can't."

Jess frowned. "Can't what?"

"Wait. It's a drop off zone." He waved his hand at the columns of traffic. "They'll give me a ticket."

Jess sighed, "Well—"

"There's a parking garage, one block over. Multi-story." He handed her a card. "Call me when you're ready."

She looked at the card. The thought of letting him drive off with the Grantlys' money in the trunk scared her, but it wasn't much different from asking him to wait at the entrance. She couldn't keep an eye on him either way.

She handed him one of her cards. "Text me when you get parked. So I know where you are."

He took the card, and shrugged. "Whatever you say."

Omar inched to a stop at the front entrance. Jess hooked her bag over her shoulder, her Glock settled inside. She tapped the back of his seat. "Don't forget, text me."

"Yeah, yeah. No problem."

She hurried along the sidewalk toward the hospital's main entrance, placing a phone call as she moved. After several rings, the operator answered.

"Antigua Hospital, David Gardner speaking. How may I help you?"

"I'm looking for Roger Grantly. He was delivered by ambulance from JFK about an hour ago. Can you tell me where I can find him?"

"One moment," Gardner replied.

# CHAPTER THIRTY-THREE

*New York City, New York*
*May 11*

LUIGI STRUGGLED TO SEE the American's limo from the rear seat of his taxi. The driver followed the American woman's vehicle along the Van Wyck Expressway to Antigua Hospital without question. He'd actually been pretty adept at staying a few cars back, but when her car turned for the hospital, his driver glared at him. "I thought you said she was cheating on you?"

Luigi briefly considered silencing the man with a bullet, but the area around the hospital was far too busy. He waved at the hospital. "He's a doctor."

His driver nodded sagely. "Ah. The worst."

The American's limo had stopped. Luigi watched as she emerged from the back seat. The driver had released the trunk from inside and she ducked half her body into the dark cavern. She was probably retrieving something from the luggage. He felt his gut tense while she rooted around in there. If she took the cash, he'd have another set of challenges and he was running out of time to dispense with them all.

When the American raised her body from the limo's deep storage, she had nothing with her except the oversized handbag he'd seen her carrying since the Orlando jet way.

His breathing returned to normal and his gut relaxed. She didn't find the ransom. Or if she did, she'd left it in place.

Which was both the good news and the bad news. Good because she didn't find it. Bad because now he had three different sites to cover.

Then again, he'd been craving excitement. Killing two old people and a small woman while carrying ten pounds of cash wasn't that challenging, but it was better than watching them from the sidelines until they reached Rome.

She slammed the trunk lid down and the limo driver pulled away.

Luigi tapped his driver's shoulder and pointed forward. "Drive past. Stop a few cars down."

Fifty feet on, his driver slowed, his indicator blinking as he waited for a minivan to pull out, leaving him a space at the curb. Luigi looked back at the American.

Her limo drove right by him. A big black Lincoln Town Car. He slid down in his seat as she watched her limo depart.

So he'd guessed correctly. She had befriended the Grantlys and enticed them to trust her with the ransom. Which meant they had also trusted her with at least some information about their son's situation. Which also meant the American was now another problem that had to be eliminated. Not ideal, but he'd handled bigger problems in this case already. He wasn't worried.

He had a small vial containing cyanide capsules in his pocket. He'd saved two for this occasion. But he hadn't expected to need more. Another elimination method would be needed for the American. A minor irritation. He was aware of the weight of the pistol in his pocket, but the possibilities for using it were limited because of his requirements.

She was small enough. He could overpower her and break her neck. An undesirable choice because he'd need to get her alone and get close enough, which he couldn't count on.

Perhaps a better option would present itself. It usually did. The only obstacles were timing and witnesses.

But he wasn't worried about those, either. He didn't worry about much of anything after all these years. He was an expert and she was nothing but a nuisance. His confidence was supported by the several million Euro bank account that proved it. He smiled again.

Prioritize. Compartmentalize. These were his strengths. The Italian made a quick decision.

Luigi handed the fare to his driver, and stepped out. The Town Car was pulling into a multi-story parking garage. She had obviously asked her driver to wait.

He turned around, but she was gone. He swore as he jogged to the front entrance. She was talking to a woman at a giant curved reception desk. A smile drew across his face. She was locating the Grantlys. She'd collected their luggage for them, and now she was returning it.

He stepped back from the entrance, keeping out of sight of the receptionist. His anger turned to lust as he watched her walk down the corridor into the building. He grinned. She had turned from a meddling irritation to an unwitting ally.

He had two options. Follow her through the hospital to the Grantlys and eliminate them now. Or give her time to leave, and find the Grantlys himself. He preferred the latter. If the old man was in a hospital room he'd be alone or maybe with his wife. The fewer people he had to deal with at one time the better.

He moved farther away from the main entrance, passed a gaggle of smokers, and stopped beside a statue where he judged he would have the best view of the entrance. The place was busy. The area's walking wounded traipsed in and out. A steady stream of ambulances stretchered in the more desperate cases.

He shuffled his weight from foot to foot, and considered joining the smokers, but he resisted. Cigarette smoke was an identifying feature. Stale tobacco smoke attached itself to clothes, skin, and hair. People latched onto it fast. They remembered the smoke, and the smoker. The last thing he wanted was anyone remembering him.

An orderly brought a man out in a wheelchair. An SUV pulled up, and the driver and the orderly helped the man into the passenger's seat. The SUV drove away.

Luigi checked his watch. He had started with plenty of time, but he wouldn't wait until the last moment. He gave the American ten more minutes, checked the knife and gun in his pockets, and headed for the reception desk.

# CHAPTER THIRTY-FOUR

JESS HURRIED THROUGH THE hospital's maze of corridors looking for the elevators. The receptionist had said Roger was on the fifth floor, the cardiac floor. She saw the elevators, and ran to catch the doors before they closed. A young couple stepped aside to let her in. A punk rocker, complete with zips and chains leaned against the rear wall, snapped chewing gum in time to the music in his head. He licked his lips as he looked at Jess, which made her skin crawl.

She was sorely tempted to take her frustration out on him, but inside a hospital, on the way to see a heart attack patient, wasn't the best place for an incident with a loaded Glock. She bit her lip. Loaded Glock. What were the laws about concealed weapons on hospital property? Not that it mattered. She had to go inside and she wouldn't leave the Glock behind. If she got stopped, Morris would fix it.

She took a deep breath and turned her back to the punker. She needed to focus. She needed to know everything the

Grantlys could tell her about the handover, about Wilson, and about the kidnappers. She needed as much from them as she could get. Because if the FBI wouldn't, or couldn't, take the Grantlys place and rescue Wilson, then she would.

If she were old, and her son was in danger, she knew that is what she would want. The Grantlys wanted the same thing, only they were from an age which left them too proud to ask.

The elevator stopped on the fifth floor. She stepped out and the doors closed, taking the punker away. The corridor was painted flat white and blindingly illuminated by too many fluorescent bulbs. Two scuffed dark lines on the floor bore witness to many years' passage of rolling hospital beds.

Her phone buzzed. She glanced at a terse message from an unknown number. B34 floor 4. Omar. *The parking garage.* She pushed the phone back in her pocket, hoping the man was as good as his word.

The cardiac care unit was easily identified by a large sign and another reception desk. She walked up to a rotund woman, brown hair, mid-sixties. "Is Roger Grantly here?"

The woman looked up at her, wearing a kindly expression. "Are you a relative?"

Jess nodded slightly, an involuntary part of the lie she had to tell. "He's my father."

The woman looked her up and down. Jess's heart beat faster. Roger as her father would be one hell of an age gap, but it was too late to take it back. She breathed in. If she screwed this up, she had no way to get to the Grantlys.

The woman opened her mouth to speak.

Jess held her hand out. "I know, I know. He's really my grandfather. They raised me. My real family," she shrugged, "you know..."

The woman's head bobbed in a slow nod. "Name?"

Jess knew she was going to ask for ID next. She had no option but to use her real name. "Jessica Kimball."

"Kimball?"

"Married name."

The woman bobbed her head again. "I think I'm going to have to check with them." She picked up her phone, and placed it back on the hook.

Jess frowned. "You can check. Give them my name. I'm sure they—"

The woman held up her hand and pointed behind Jess.

A nurse wearing a nameplate identifying her as Denise Shaw was guiding Mrs. Grantly along the corridor.

Jess smiled. "Harriet."

Mrs. Grantly waved but her eyes focused well beyond Jess.

Jess held her hand out. Harriet took it.

Jess looked at Nurse Shaw. "How is he doing?"

The nurse smiled. "Are you a relative?"

Harriet held Jess's hand and said, "It's all right. She's with me."

"He's had a heart attack. Possibly two." Nurse Shaw breathed deeply. "He's on oxygen and nitro. We're prepping him for angioplasty."

"You're going to operate?" Harriet's tone was calm, simply seeking information.

"It's a small procedure. We'll put a stent in, to open his arteries. So he'll get better blood flow." The kindly Nurse Shaw patted Harriet's hand. "He'll feel better."

"When will they do the procedure?"

"Soon. It'll only take an hour. But you won't be able to see him until the morning. Do you live nearby?"

Jess shook her head.

"I'd recommend you find a hotel." Nurse Shaw squeezed Harriet's hand and looked directly at Jess. "I have the feeling traveling to New York was a little more than they're used to."

Jess wrapped her arm around Harriet's shoulder. "We'll be okay, won't we?"

Harriet nodded, and the nurse left them.

Jess steered Harriet to the elevator. "How about something to eat before we look for a hotel?"

Harriet leaned close to Jess. "Where are our bags?"

Jess smiled. "They're okay. I have a car."

She whispered, "But the money?"

"It's okay," Jess said. "It's perfectly safe."

# CHAPTER THIRTY-FIVE

LUIGI STOOD NEAR THE hospital entrance, the curved reception desk in front of him. He bit his lip. The American woman had walked this way. She had stood where he stood, talked to the receptionist, and disappeared deeper into the building.

He remembered her body as he'd followed behind, the swing of her hips and the bounce of her blonde curls.

He spun on his heels, and walked out of the hospital. She hadn't been carrying the suitcases. Her driver had loaded them into the limo, and she had got out without them. Could she have been so stupid as to trust her driver with the money?

He jogged toward the multi-story car park. There was only one place the money could be. He followed the roadway into the building, scanning the signs for limo parking. There was no such sign. He swore. He couldn't be that lucky. He would have to search the whole building.

He checked his gun, and jogged a path around the first floor.

## CHAPTER THIRTY-FIVE

# CHAPTER THIRTY-SIX

JESS SETTLED HARRIET IN a seat in the corner of the hospital café, and joined the line at the counter for food. She returned with coffee and cake on a tray. Harriet was knitting what looked like baby boots. She didn't notice as Jess placed the tray on the table, and divided the drinks and cake between them.

"Coffee?" she said.

Harriet looked up, her hands still turning cotton yarn into baby clothes. She nodded.

Jess sat. "He's in the best place."

Harriet frowned.

"Roger."

The woman gave an exaggerated nod. "Yes. But not Wilson."

Jess bit her lip.

Harriet's hands slowed their pace.

"Everyone is doing their best. For Roger, and for Wilson."

Behind her thick glasses, Harriet's eyes widened. "Oh, my dear. I didn't mean to sound ungrateful."

"It's okay, Harriet." Jess touched the woman's arm. "You've been under a lot of stress."

Her hands stopped their knitting. "What's going to happen?"

Jess took a deep breath. "You can't go, Harriet. Roger needs you, and…you're not really up to dealing with a gang of kidnappers."

The woman's head slumped forward. "No. No, we're not. We thought…" She shook her head. "I don't know what we thought. We just had to help Wilson when he needed us."

"I understand. Everyone understands. We will do our utmost to get your son back."

Harriet frowned. "We, who?"

"Me. And the FBI."

Harriet stood up, her knitting slipping to the floor. "No."

Jess frowned. "Yes." She curled up one side of her lips. "Maybe even the State Department."

"No, no. They can't."

Jess stood, and held Harriet by the arm. "Yes. This isn't something one person can—"

Harriet waved her hands. "No, no, no. You don't understand. They can't. They mustn't."

Jess frowned. "Mustn't what?"

Harriet grabbed Jess's arms, one hand on each. "They mustn't…The FBI. They told us not to go to the police."

"Harriet—"

"They'll kill him. They said so."

"They won't know until it's too late for them."

The woman shook her head. "They will, they will."

"Harriet—"

"They've been watching us."

Jess's skin tingled. Her mouth hung open. "What?"

"They've been watching us. They have."

"The kidnappers?"

Harriet nodded fast. "They told us things. Like when we went shopping."

Jess frowned. "Shopping?"

Harriet nodded. "They're watching us."

"You've met them?"

Harriet shook her head. She picked up her bag and upturned it on the table, the contents spilling over the tray and the cakes. She sifted through the wool and the patterns and a hundred other items, and pulled out a small purple mobile phone. "They've been calling us."

Jess took the phone. It was switched off. "I thought you didn't have a mobile phone."

Harriet shook her head. "We don't. They sent that. In the mail."

Jess glanced at the garish pay-as-you-go phone. "You've been answering it?"

Harriet nodded. "They called last night."

"Have they called today?"

Harriet shook her head. "I don't know. I turned it off. Like the flight attendant said."

Jess looked at the tiny blank screen. She hovered her thumb over the power button. The kidnappers had been watching the Grantlys. They knew what Roger and Harriet were doing. They knew what was happening. Maybe they even knew about Roger's heart attack.

She looked around the café. They could be anyone and anywhere.

She took a deep breath, and held the power button down until a logo appeared and the phone registered a cellular connection. The phone dinged. There were three missed calls.

Jess looked at Harriet.

Harriet looked back. "Do you think they're here?"

Goosebumps crawled all over Jess's skin. She grabbed Harriet's arm. "Stay here. Right here. With lots of people. Don't go anywhere. Stay with lots of people. Out in the open. You understand?"

"What—"

Jess shook Harriet's arm. "Here. Lots of people. Understand?"

"All right, dear. But—"

Jess turned and ran.

# CHAPTER THIRTY-SEVEN

IT TOOK LONGER TO locate her limo than Luigi expected. He jogged up the incline to the fourth floor of the parking garage. He sweated under his jacket. The cars had thinned out as he climbed the levels, but still he had to circle each floor to be sure he didn't miss the Lincoln.

It was a large garage with plenty of full-sized black sedans. He'd wasted time checking out a couple that turned out to be Crown Victorias. It was all he could do not to shoot out the tires in frustration.

He slowed to a walk, breathing hard. He needed to bring his heart rate down. His aim would twitch in time to the heavy beat of his heart. He needed to be ready for when he found the car.

The parking levels were divided into symmetrical halves. He took the left half first. It was closer to the exit ramp, and if the driver had any experience, he would want to be quick out of the parking lot and back to earning money.

He started at the low bay numbers and worked his way up.

With a random chance of finding the car, it made no difference whether he worked up or down, but he was a methodical man, and his methods had always paid off.

When he found her limo, he approached behind the cover of parked vehicles and structural support poles until he could see the driver through the side window.

The driver had reclined the seat and lay back almost flat. His arm was bent at the elbow and covered his eyes. The limo's engine was not running.

Luigi approached silently until he was standing next to the vehicle. He rapped his knuckles on the window.

The driver jerked his arm away, startled. When he looked up, Luigi gestured to request the driver lower his window and simultaneously said, "Please, sir?"

The driver lowered the window.

*Americans. Idiots.*

When the window was fully retracted, Luigi brought his hand from behind his back, lifted the pistol and placed two quick rounds in the center of his forehead.

The driver slumped sideways. Luigi put a third round in his left temple. Insurance. *Always better to be certain.*

Luigi returned the gun to his pocket, reached into the cabin and unlocked the door. He pulled the driver from the vehicle and dragged him to the back of the limo. He'd released the trunk and hefted the dead weight of his body into the deep storage.

The American woman hadn't inspected the contents of old man Grantly's suitcase because it was locked. Luigi smiled. *Americans locked everything. And then trusted those locks to hold.*

He would miss working in this country. Where else would he find so many gullible people concentrated in one place again?

He pulled out the box cutter he'd removed from his locker at the airport and sliced the green luggage belt and allowed the excess pressure of the stuffed luggage to push the lid open on the ancient hinges. He slid the box cutter back into his pocket and rifled through the contents.

Within five seconds, he found the first set of bills inside a quart-sized plastic baggie. Stacked neatly in a one-inch packet and wrapped with a paper money wrapper. The top and bottom bills on the stack were $100 denominations. If the entire packet consisted of $100 bills, then the set of fifty bills totaled $50,000. In which case there should be four packages of fifty and a fifth package containing twenty-four bills. If the denominations were smaller, he would find more packages.

In less than a minute, Luigi found six. He pulled the baggies out and stuffed them into his pockets. The bulges were noticeable if someone was paying attention, but at the moment, he had no alternatives.

He closed the trunk lid with the driver's body inside. He turned and moved toward the limo's cabin.

Then he heard a woman shout, "Stop!"

# CHAPTER THIRTY-EIGHT

JESS BURST OUT OF the hospital elevator on the ground floor, and ran. She mashed the redial button on her phone, and held the device against her ear. The exit doors opened automatically as she approached. She slowed to a fast walk as the call connected.

Morris came on the line. "Jess?"

"They're here. They're in the country. The kidnappers. They've been watching the Grantlys."

"Jess, Jess. Slow down. How do you know?"

She took a deep breath, pulled the strap of her messenger bag tighter on her shoulder, and walked to the multi-story garage. "Harriet told me. They sent the Grantlys a burner phone, and they've been calling on it."

"Since when?"

"Few days. Plus, I think they've called since Roger had his heart attack."

"What's the number?"

"What?" She stopped and stamped her foot on the ground.

"Damn!" She took a deep breath, and looked back at the hospital entrance. "I didn't get it. Harriet still has the phone."

"Where is she?"

"In the hospital."

"And where are you?"

"Heading back to my car."

"Go back and stay with her. We'll be there in ten minutes."

"No. Listen, I left their money in their luggage. It's in the back of my car."

"Jess, never mind the money, go back—"

"If the kidnappers know the money is in the luggage—"

"Maybe they do, maybe they don't—"

"If they get the money, they won't need to keep Wilson alive. And they'll vanish. We'll be back to square one. More people will lose their lives."

"Jess, please. We're two miles away. I have four men and a team from Brooklyn. Don't do anything stupid."

"Harriet's in the hospital café, and I'll be in the parking garage across the street. Fourth floor. B34." She punched the off button, and ran.

The garage entrance was wide, two lanes in and out. Ramps led to the upper floors, one an entrance spiral, the other the exit. A concrete walkway led to an elevator. There were two buttons, large off white plastic arrows, one up, one down. She punched the up button. It didn't light up. She pressed the button harder, holding it in, pushing it sideways. There was no response.

She wrapped the strap to her bag over her head, and took the stairs. The staircase was dark, filthy, and overwhelmed by the acrid odor of urine. The only light spilled in through openings from the streetlights on the road below.

She worked her way up one floor, watching the corners,

doorways, and shadows for movement. Far off in the building, metal creaked. Her skin crawled.

She put her hand in her bag, and wrapped her fingers around the grip of her Glock, resting her trigger finger on the guard. She kept the gun inside the bag, close enough to use, if it came to that.

She moved up the floors until she reached a large numeral four painted on the wall. A big heavy steel door hung low on its hinges. A small square window offered a view into the parking area. She peered through.

She was near the exit ramp. The cars seemed scattered at random around the floor. She saw no one.

She pushed the heavy door open. It scraped along the concrete floor, squealing like nails on a blackboard.

The garage was quiet. Eerily quiet. Fluorescent lights washed the parking area with a harsh yellow glow. The cars weren't parked randomly at all. They were clustered around one corner of the floor, near the exit. A sign on the closest pillar read A0. She looked down the row of cars. The next pillar read A10.

Omar's Town Car was at the far end. She walked diagonally across the line of cars, and saw the big black Lincoln at the end of the row, backed into the parking spot. A man stood beside the car. Omar stretching his legs, perhaps?

Before she could call his name the man bent down. There was a flash of light inside the car. A hard, solid chug thumped through the air. The cycle repeated again and again. Flash, chug. Flash, chug.

Jess froze, her mouth open, ready to call to Omar. She had one foot in the air. Her lungs locked up.

She clamped her mouth shut, fighting back an instinct to scream. She forced her legs backward, moving between two cars.

She dipped low beside a thick concrete pillar.

Omar? The man had shot him at point blank range. He hadn't stood a chance. She clenched her fist, and realized she was holding her Glock. She slid off her bag, laid it on the ground, and pulled out her phone.

Through the glass of the parked cars, she could see the man moving to the rear of the Lincoln. The driver's door was open. The man was struggling. He had to be carrying the body. The trunk popped up, and the man turned to lift Omar's dead body into the cavernous space.

When he turned, she saw him, head on. He wore jeans and a blazer. His clothes looked like he'd slept in them, and he looked unshaven. She glowered at him. The man from the airport. The one who had been staring at her. The one on the plane. She felt cold.

She pressed the mute switch on her phone, and called Morris. She spoke as soon as he picked up. "Morris. I'm on the fourth floor. Column B34. At the back of the garage. The kidnapper is here. He just shot my driver, and I'd guess he's taking the money."

"Stay down, Jess. Stay out of the way. We're almost there. Three minutes, tops."

The man closed the limo's trunk and straightened his jacket.

"I don't think we have three minutes."

"Jess—"

"Fourth floor. At the back. Hurry." She hung up.

If he left with the money, he wouldn't need Wilson Grantly alive any more. He would kill Wilson. Or his accomplices would. No good outcome was possible if this man got away.

She checked her Glock and moved a couple of cars closer to the limo.

He closed the driver's door. His pockets bulged, his jacket ballooned around him. He walked away from the limo. He passed one car, two, three.

Jess held her gun out. "Stop!"

He stopped and looked in her direction. It was a natural reaction. A quirk of nature. Walking people generally obeyed instructions, running people usually ran harder. He looked calm and serene. Happy, even.

"Lie down," she said.

He didn't move. He wasn't moving but he wasn't taking orders from her, either.

She gestured with the Glock. "On the ground. Now!"

He leaned forward, as if bowing, as if he was going to lie in the concrete dust on the floor. And sprang back up. Gun out. Chest height. A pistol with a silencer. Pointed directly at her.

Jess jumped back. She folded herself in two, pivoted and lunged behind a concrete pillar. The man fired. It was like the car. The same flashes of light. The same chug, chug beating the air. Concrete chips exploded above her head.

Her heart raced. She panted, her mouth wide open.

He was fifty feet away. From behind the pillar, she couldn't see him.

She remembered the words of the man who had first taught her how to use a gun. Lose sight, lose the fight.

She took a deep breath. She gripped her Glock with both hands, and leapt from behind the concrete pillar to behind the engine block of an SUV.

He fired. The windscreen of the SUV exploded. She gripped her gun, and squeezed the trigger. One. Two. The Glock boomed. Louder and heavier than his silenced pistol.

The man ducked and fired. A wild shot hit the garage roof

and brought down a cloud of concrete.

She crouched down, keeping her eyes a fraction above the glass beltline of the SUV, and the man in view.

He ran, doubled over, awkward steps, his bulbous jacket flapping hard left and firm right. He was going for the limo. Omar's keys were probably still in the ignition.

Jess angled the gun down the side of the SUV. He would come into view. She tensed her finger on the trigger. She could see the nose of the limo. If she could just stop him, Morris would arrive and take over. She hoped.

She saw a blur. Jacket, jeans, loafers. She squeezed. Aiming ahead of him. The Glock boomed, jolting in her hands. She held it down. Resisting the urge to let the barrel rise as the recoil wanted it to do. She needed her next shot to be on target if she was going to fire again.

The man screamed. Short, sharp, guttural. Pain and shock, tightly controlled.

She heard a thump, and peered around the side of the SUV. He was folded over, one hand on his side, the other on the Lincoln. He shuffled toward the driver's door.

She inched forward. If she shot now, she would hit him for sure. He was prone. Stationary. No longer a moving target. Sandwiched between the Lincoln and the next car.

But she wasn't a killer. She'd hit him when she only meant to frighten him into submission. And if she killed him, Morris might never learn where Wilson Grantly was hidden.

Omar's killer was still moving, but not easily. Morris wasn't far away. She eased back behind the inadequate safety of the SUV's engine block and waited.

The door to the Lincoln popped open. She heard grunting. The door slammed.

There was silence and then the churning of the starter motor.

The Lincoln leapt forward, tires screeching, the rear fishtailing out of the parking space. She whipped her gun into the gap between the SUV and the next car.

The Lincoln passed her. A streak of black. And gone.

She leapt up. The Lincoln made a wild turn at the end of the row of parked cars. He was heading for the exit.

She ran full out for the stairwell, taking the steps three and four at a time, crashing her shoulder into the wall to slow her for the turns.

She skipped the third floor, and hit the door to the second level at full speed, ramming the door back against the concrete.

The Lincoln raced down the exit ramp. She ran toward it, her Glock in front of her.

The Lincoln lurched left, following the arrow for the exit. She took the turn, sprinting after the Lincoln's red taillights.

He turned another corner. She heard a loud crash. The impact of metal and glass. An engine roared. Tires squealed. Another crash.

She reached the bottom of the ramp. The Lincoln was sideways across the lane, its nose buried in a minivan reversing out of its parking spot, and its rear wedged against a concrete pillar.

Sirens sounded. Harsh and loud and close.

The man was in the Lincoln, hands still on the wheel.

Jess walked forward, her gun trained on the man, keeping behind him.

A woman pulled two girls from the minivan.

Jess made eye contact. "Move! Go! Get away!"

The woman caught sight of the Glock, and needed no more encouragement, hustling her children away.

The Lincoln's engine died. The man stumbled out.

Jess took cover behind a pillar, her Glock in her outstretched arm.

He waved his gun, and stumbled to one knee.

Jess kept her Glock on him. "Down!"

He swung his gun in her direction. She whipped behind the safety of the concrete as he loosed a hail of bullets. Glass exploded and fragments of the pillar flew around her. She squeezed her arms to her sides.

His gun clicked.

The bullets stopped.

She stepped out from the pillar, Glock first. "Drop it!"

He threw the gun at her. It clattered across the ground. He gripped his side, and rolled onto his back, breathing in hard, gasping.

She stepped forward, and kicked his gun away. "You hear those sirens? They're for you."

He sneered.

She kept the Glock pointed directly at his head.

The sirens grew louder, ricocheting oddly from the building's corners and walls. She sighed. They were in the garage. Morris was close.

The man lurched. He stuffed his hand in his jacket pocket.

She leapt back, closer to the pillar. "Move and I shoot!"

The man spat at her.

Three big black government issued SUVs screeched to a stop on the other side of the minivan. Morris was first out. He leapt over the hood of the Lincoln, a massive revolver unflinchingly trained on the man on the ground.

Morris looked at her. "Any more?"

She shook her head, and swallowed. "No."

A swarm of agents followed Morris, splitting up, spreading out, and weapons ready. Two of them cuffed the man on the ground.

Morris holstered his gun. "You okay?"

She nodded.

He looked at the Glock. "Will you put that down?"

She stared at her outstretched arms, her gun still trained on the man. She exhaled, and lowered the weapon.

Morris watched the gun drop to her side, and gave her a flat smile. "Thank you."

Jess nodded to the man. "He was at Orlando airport, on the flight, and at JFK. He shot my driver."

Morris frowned.

"That was my car. I left the money in the trunk. He shot my driver, and took the money." Jess swallowed. "He put Omar in the trunk."

An agent popped the trunk. Jess couldn't see inside, but she guessed he searched for a pulse before nodding to Morris. Morris whistled.

An ambulance and two NYPD patrol cars pulled up behind the government SUVs.

"Everything's under control." Morris took Jess by the elbow. "Let's get you out of here."

# CHAPTER THIRTY-NINE

*New York City, New York*
*May 11*
*10:00 PM*

AT MORRIS'S INSTRUCTION, TWO NYPD cops escorted Jess to the hospital café. Harriet was still there, knitting. She gasped as Jess relayed the events of the past twenty minutes. No sooner had Jess finished her story than a nurse arrived, told them Roger was recovering well from surgery, and took Harriet off to find a hotel.

Jess rummaged through her bag. The crime scene investigation team had taken her Glock. She felt naked without it, her double cop escort notwithstanding.

Her muscles ached from the exertion and the stress. She stretched out and sat back down, but she couldn't relax. The café chairs had been chosen because they were indestructible, not comfortable.

She checked her first class ticket to Rome. *Taboo Magazine* had bought a non-refundable e-ticket. Cheaper, but, as the name implied, no refund if it wasn't used. She grinned. Rome was one of the great cities of the world. It would be criminal to let it go to waste. Besides, she'd planned a couple of days' recuperation. No reason not to recuperate in Rome.

Morris arrived. He sat opposite her in the almost deserted café, and made a constant string of phone calls. She caught snippets. Several names went by. The word Rome came up on most calls. RCMP and Canada were popular, too. Finally, he put his phone on the table.

"All sorted?" she said.

He gave a flat smile.

She waited as long as she could. "What?"

"The Italians found the payphone and went through the farm with a fine tooth comb. Nothing. No Wilson Grantly. And nothing to suggest the farm was involved with any of the Blazek team."

She exhaled. "So, we're back to the planned exchange at the Rome airport. Otherwise, you'll never catch these guys. Or find Wilson Grantly."

Morris shrugged.

"You're going to do something, aren't you?"

He nodded to his phone. "What do you think I've been doing?"

"What's his name?"

"The man you shot?"

She nodded.

"We found a key in his pocket. Fitted to a locker at JFK. We found a passport with the name Luigi Ficarra to match a ticket to Rome on Flight 12 tonight."

"You believe it?"

He grimaced. "We're running prints and DNA and checking databases, but we can't exactly ask him."

She frowned.

He cleared his throat. "He's dead."

Her skin tingled. She bolted out of her chair, scraping it back across the floor.

He reached his hand out. "It's okay, he—"

"I killed him?" Her entire body had begun to shiver.

Morris shook his head. "Cyanide."

She stared at him.

"Your bullet wouldn't have killed him."

She sank back into her seat, and clamped her jaw shut.

"Forensics and an autopsy will prove it, but the doctor on the scene was positive."

She exhaled loudly. "So, is that it for the Blazek crime ring? The Italian connection? Cyanide suicides?"

Morris shook his head again. "The whole kidnap and ransom thing is a team effort. Assuming our man was Luigi, he has a brother. Enzo. The Mounties believe Enzo murdered Marek and his wife. Shot her while nursing their baby."

"I heard." Jess grimaced, and wrapped her arms around her.

"Sick bastard, for sure. Probably even worse than Luigi, who was no Mother Teresa." Morris nodded and drained the cup of black coffee he'd brought to the table. "And we still have to get Wilson Grantly back."

"But you have a plan?"

"Oh, I have a plan. But there's a lot of people involved now. A lot more to coordinate. More hoops and red tape."

"The Grantlys are depending on us."

"Us?"

"I promised Harriet."

He sighed. "Don't get me wrong, Jess. You've done a wonderful job, and we wouldn't have reopened this case without you." He looked at his hands then back at her. "We really do appreciate everything you've done." He frowned. "But we'll take it from here. I can give you an exclusive for *Taboo* when we get everything wrapped up. How's that?"

She looked at him. His back straight, his shoulders square, the scar on his lip a shade redder than she remembered.

She knew his pain. They were on the same side of law and order, and crime and justice. She reported raw and painful stories, highlighting the victims, and sometimes...sometimes, bringing some measure of justice.

But he took on the criminals, the drug lords, and the gangs. He put together links, and patterns, and traces. The world only saw the moments of fame on television broadcasts, but behind them, she knew his days were filled mostly with perspiration, sometimes with inspiration, and for one tiny fraction of a percent, pure terror.

"Okay. Sure. That'll work. Glad I could help." She watched his face, trying to determine whether he believed her. "I wouldn't have it any other way. I'm not cut out for gunfights. I really do believe the pen is mightier than the sword."

"Thanks, Jess." He grinned and raised his empty cup in a salute. "I owe you."

She stretched her legs out. "Oh, yeah. I wore out my shoe leather on this case." She turned her toes up in her shoes. "I almost forgot."

He snorted a laugh. "Sure. I owe you. Send me the bill."

"No." She leaned over the table and smiled. "Get them for someone else." She tapped his wedding band. "I think she deserves them."

He looked at her, his face a mask. He opened his mouth, as if to speak, but stood, instead. "Thank you...I'll tell her."

He cleared his throat. "I have to get going. I'll handle things with the NYPD. You're free to go."

She stood. "Good. Because I have a first class ticket that I don't want to waste."

He gazed at her, his eyebrows down, and his head tilted forward a fraction. "You've done your bit, Jess. Leave Enzo Ficarra, and whatever else we find in Italy, to us and the Italians, okay?"

She held out her hand. "I have plenty of things on my to-do list. Don't worry."

He cocked his head and gave her a skeptical look for a few moments before he relaxed and shook her hand. "I'll get your Glock back to you as soon as I can."

He walked out of the café, his phone already against his ear.

She wasn't concerned about misleading him. He'd find out soon enough. But if she'd been straight about her plans, he could have prevented her from getting on the plane. This was one of those situations where forgiveness was easier to get than permission.

She waited until Morris left before she picked up her messenger bag, and followed him outside. She needed sleep and a decent meal, but she wasn't worried, she'd get both in a first class seat across the Atlantic.

Her shoulders ached, and her feet were sore. She was almost sorry she had turned down Morris's offer of new shoes.

Fifty feet ahead of her, Morris turned right, back to the parking garage and the crime scene investigation. She turned left, and waited in a line for a taxi.

He was a good man, and a good agent. Together they had stopped one-half of a crime ring. But only the first half. The second half waited in Italy. Enzo Ficarra. Luigi's brother.

She exhaled. Morris might have it covered. The Italians might be there to handle things. Wilson might be rescued. But it was all might, might, might. And as Morris said, there were more hoops and red tape involved now.

She wasn't good with red tape. She wanted results. She owed it to Omar, who was only doing his job, to the people who had lost their lives and the ones who had lost their life savings, and most of all to Roger and Harriet.

She had promised to help them get their son back.

That was exactly what she planned to do. How would she accomplish that without the ransom money? *Taboo*. *Taboo* might pay. At least temporarily, until she could get the Grantlys' money back from Morris.

A taxi pulled up. "JFK," she said as she climbed in the back. The taxi's tires chirped when the cab drove away. She watched the billboards and the neons and the streetlights race by and clenched her fists.

Tomorrow, Enzo Ficarra was expecting an American to get off Flight 12 to meet him at the airport for the hostage exchange. She wouldn't disappoint him.

She'd have to hustle to make it, but she absolutely would not miss her midnight flight.

She didn't.

### THE END

*Enjoy an excerpt from the next
Jess Kimball Thriller.*

# FATAL ERROR

**by DIANE CAPRI**

# CHAPTER ONE

*Tuscany, Italy*
*May 12*

A DOG BARKED, LONELY in the night. The sound rolled down the hill. Echoing over the lawn. From the house at the top, to the woods at the bottom. It was more a timorous complaint than a demand for attention. The kind of sound made by the upper half of a body. Short. Thin. High pitched. Pushed out with an expectation of kindness borne from years of loving attention. Enzo Ficarra smiled. It was not the growl of a broad rib cage and strong lungs. It was not a big dog.

The sound quelled the last of his concerns.

He had scheduled this meeting for the following day. They would not be expecting him a day early. They would not be prepared to fight.

He walked slowly up the hill. Measured steps. Neither rushing nor sauntering. The walk of a guest expecting to be welcomed. Deception and surprise were the stock of his trade, and he walked to deceive any eyes that might be upon him. Surprise would come soon enough.

The house had square walls and round balconies. Wrought iron railings decorated the windows. Eaves hung out from the building. Arched tiles covered the roof.

It was a traditional Tuscan home. Around the house was perhaps an acre of garden. Enough to give the occupants their privacy. Enough to keep his visit private, too.

He reached the rear door into the kitchen. Deep inside the house, a television played. A mindless show host asking mindless questions of a mindless audience.

They weren't expecting him. Which was as it should have been, the night before the meeting.

All was well.

He braced a flat metal hook against the doorframe. Three occupants inside. Fifteen rounds in his Beretta. More than enough to do the job. He would act fast. Not that he was concerned they would fight back.

Which might be interesting.

Still, best avoided.

He savored the moment. Long ago, he had learned to crave adrenaline. The chemical that quavered other's voices, deepened his. What trembled other's hands and fingers, steadied his. He was never more focused than when events promised a rush.

Tonight should be such a time.

He pulled his silenced Beretta from his pocket, and took a deep breath.

He shoved his weight behind the metal hook. Its sharp edge cut into the wood. Splintered the doorframe. Opened a gap to the lock.

He felt the solid touch of metal. He wrenched the hook down. Pulling at the lock. Tearing at the screws. Wrenching them from the cracked remains of the doorframe.

He barreled forward. All his weight. Shoulder first.

Glass shattered. The lock clattered across a tiled floor.

The door flew back.

He scanned his gun across the room. Left to right. Kitchen counters. Gas stove. Refrigerator.

No one there.

He kicked the door closed.

A middle-aged woman appeared at the doorway into the living room, dressed in her nightgown.

She froze, her eyes wide, and her mouth open. Fear overwhelmed her capacity for thought.

He leveled the Beretta and fired.

The silencer muted the gun's roar. Still loud. Still forceful. Still a soundtrack to hot metal and death.

The woman tumbled back.

Enzo stepped over the body.

The living room was empty. A single shot silenced the television.

He darted through the door to the hall.

A man stood on the bottom of the stairs, a briefcase clutched to his chest. Ten years older than the woman. Unhealthy, too. Michael Taviani, Mike to his now-dead American wife, Lane. He thrust the briefcase forward. "Please. I have it!"

Enzo glanced up. The stairs were unoccupied.

Mike edged closer. The case still in front of him. Like a shield. "Please?"

Enzo gestured to the living room. Mike stepped through. He gasped at the sight of his wife, motionless on the floor.

Enzo closed the door, sealing the living room from the hallway.

Mike swallowed. His voice trembled. "You said tomorrow. The meeting—"

"I'm here now."

Mike stared at his dead wife. "But—"

"I make the rules, Taviani. You know this."

Mike's mouth opened and closed. A goldfish. Overwhelmed. Unable to comprehend where he'd gone wrong. Unable to grasp the events occurring around him.

Enzo pointed the Beretta toward a low coffee table. "Open it."

Mike placed the briefcase on the table. The latch thumped open. He lifted the lid. "A quarter million euro. Like you s aid."

"Show me."

The notes were wrapped in bundles. Mike lifted out a handful. Ten thousand euros. Maybe twenty.

Enzo waved a flashlight over them. A black light. Plenty of ultraviolet energy to excite photons, and reveal invisible marks. These notes kept their muted colors. The subtle blues and reds and greens that thwarted casual counterfeiters. But he wasn't worried about counterfeits. Mike wasn't quite that skilled, or clever. The black light assuaged a different concern. The notes were not marked for tracing.

Mike had followed instructions, as expected.

"Close it," Enzo said.

Mike complied. He held out the briefcase.

Glass crunched.

Enzo spun toward the noise. The wife lay dead as before.

Mike dived for Enzo. "Run!"

Enzo leapt sideways, pointing the Beretta and squeezing the trigger at the same time.

The gun seemed to boom louder than before in the silent house.

Mike twitched and jerked. His legs gave out from under him. His arms flailed.

He tumbled past Enzo. Head first onto the carpet and into his own rapidly pooling blood, which flowed steadily while his heart continued to pump.

Enzo glimpsed a thin figure in the kitchen. The daughter. A teenager. Over-indulged, to be sure. Seventeen now.

She had been the one who answered Enzo's original email containing fake pleas for help. She'd responded to the sleazy pitch asking for money to save young girls her age from human trafficking. Of course, seventeen-year-olds had no money. But through her, he'd reached her parents' bank account.

He shook his head. Parents would do almost anything for their children. Even when the children were the cause of their troubles.

Tears marked her cheeks. Her eyes wide. Standing by the rear door.

Enzo ran to the kitchen.

She backed away from the door. He leveled his gun on her. Her eyes darted to one side. Behind him. The briefest glimpse, like the recognition of movement.

He spun, training the Beretta to the living room doorway. The space was empty. Blood had also pooled around the woman. She hadn't moved. Nor would she. Her husband was not so lucky.

Mike rolled on the floor holding his stomach. Still alive. For a few moments more.

Enzo spun back to the girl but she had vanished.

He pressed his face against the kitchen window, scanning the moonlit garden.

He heard a click to his right. Another door.

He raced to twist the handle. Locked.

He leaned his shoulder into the door. It was solid.

He stepped back and fired at the lock twice. The wood splintered and danced.

He swung his boot up, kicking hard. The door snapped open, slamming back against the wall.

A laundry room. A washer and dryer along one wall. Washing powders and laundry stacked on a work surface along the other. A closed window at the far end. No girl. And no way out.

He glanced behind the door. Nothing.

He eased down, peering into the glass of the washing machine. It seemed impossible to think she could have squeezed into such a close space, but he'd seen fear motivate people to remarkable feats.

The washer was empty.

He moved into the crowded room. His back to the work surface. He passed the washer. Passed the gap between the washer and dryer.

The dryer's large door was metal. No doubt with a firm spring latch. He would have heard it open and close.

He adjusted his grip on the gun and moved past the dryer, to the space between its white metal side and the end of the room.

A narrow space. Long and thin. Like the girl.

She had contorted her body. Knees, shoulders, legs. Twisted. Cramped. Painful. Her head angled sideways. Her eyes staring. He leveled his gun on her. She had been brave and quick. With her dash to hide when she first saw him from the kitchen, she might even have had a bright future in front of her. In another world. Not the one in which she lived.

He took a deep breath. At another time, he might even feel he should recruit her. But not here. Not now. She had seen his face. She knew who he was. He lived not far from this very home.

He had no choice. He'd known that weeks ago. Her foolish parents should have known it, too.

Her breathing was ragged. Hard work for her lungs in such confines. He turned his face away, fired twice, and spared her lungs the work.

He didn't look back. He closed the laundry room door behind him. It drifted open again, the lock gone. He stepped over the woman's body, and into the living room.

Mike had dragged himself up against a chair. He struggled to dial the old-fashioned phone.

Enzo fired twice more. He placed the shots together. Quick succession. Center of Mike's forehead. His lifeless torso slumped sideways. The phone tumbled to the floor.

Enzo jerked the phone from the wall. He returned the money to the briefcase, and closed the latches.

The meeting had not gone as smoothly as he'd planned. Such conditions meant unacceptable levels of evidence.

He returned to the kitchen, placed the sugar bowl in the microwave, and set it for ten minutes. As the microwave hummed, he turned the four gas burners to full open positions. He tucked the case under his arm and left, closing the door behind him.

He returned to his spot in the trees at the bottom of the garden to wait. The minutes ticked by.

Before the microwave timer finished, the sugar caught fire. Flames escaped the microwave and the gas ignited. Not with Hollywood flamboyance, but a smooth, relentless *whoosh*. Here, in the countryside, with neighbors miles away, no one would find the fire until it had run its course.

The fuel burned easily in the oxygen-rich mixture. Fingers of fire reached through the doors and windows.

The dog he'd heard barking earlier ran from the rear door. Small legs. Leaping more than running. Wisps of smoke trailed from its fur. It ran to the woods, and rolled in the grass.

The fire grew to the second floor. First, a yellow glow in the windows then roaring flames that spilled out of window frames and lapped upward.

The dog trotted to sit beside him.

Enzo watched the fire until flames burst through the roof. The dog stared at him expectantly, and barked.

His brother, Luigi, was returning today from New York. One last ransom to collect in Rome this afternoon. One last family to terminate tonight. After that, vacation. He'd promised his wife and his children. He'd been working too much. Luigi, too.

Enzo picked up the case, and left the dog alone and lonely in the dark.

# CHAPTER TWO

*Tuscany, Italy*
*May 12*

A FEW HOURS LATER, Enzo Ficarra sipped his espresso as dawn crept over the horizon behind him. A cheap cell phone lay on his patio table. The battery was fully charged, the shrill buzzer was set to its loudest volume, and the display showed five bars. But none of those things mattered. The one person who knew the number had not called. His brother, Luigi.

He stood the phone upright, and tapped his fingers on the table while the rising sun shortened long shadows. The phone kept its silence.

A gull's caw drew his attention eastwards, across the deep green lawn, down the rocks that led to the shore, and out over the sea. A trawler sailed by, heading for port in the next town, gulls diving in its wake to pick off the scraps.

He sipped his third espresso.

Scraps.

He took a deep breath.

Not for him.

He had a good business. It worked well. People were basically honest. They wanted to believe that of other people, too. It was a useful trait. Gullibility was how he manipulated them. And the older they were, the more they believed, and the easier they were to manipulate.

He finished his drink.

Like any business, contracts were contracts. Agreements had to be honored. He never failed his responsibilities, and he expected his clients to do the same. But when they did not, the rules had to be enforced.

He rolled the still warm demitasse cup between his palms, and watched the dregs of golden foam run around the bottom of the cup.

Enzo placed the white china cup securely on its saucer. The cup was a trophy of sorts, he supposed. He'd collected the set from Marek's club in Montreal, *Les Canard*. What a miserable day that had been. Wet, cold. Betrayal by an old friend, which was the worst kind. He shuddered.

Marek caused an unfortunate disruption to their profitable business. Contracts had been broken, agreements breached, a lapse in confidence. The enterprise was shut down and loose ends were wrapped up.

A petty incident that demanded the utmost care to bring about the final, successful conclusion. So his brother, Luigi, had travelled to Florida to collect the last payment, a quarter of a million dollars. The Italian economy being what it was, a quarter of a million American dollars would fatten their ailing bottom line nicely.

Luigi was fast, strong, and an excellent shot. More than

once, he had worked for days on the most meager of sleep. He had escaped situations that would have overwhelmed ordinary men, and returned to tell the tale.

Forcing the old couple to bring their life savings to Rome to exchange it for their son's life should have been a simple matter for his brother.

Boarding a plane was a tedious process. Check-in lines. Security guards on minimum wages. Jet bridges with passenger lines wide and long. Sniveling children, frightened mothers, bored pilots prone to error.

He tamped down his annoyance. His brother would have been patient. He would have stood in line. He would have had his ticket ready, his passport in hand. He would have smiled at the check-in attendant, and complied with security nonsense without complaint. He would have answered questions with a smile. A model passenger. Accepting. Accommodating. Anonymous.

And before he departed for Rome, he would have called.

Enzo turned the phone over in his hands. Flight 12 had left New York hours ago. His brother was either on it, or he was not. Plain and simple. But with no phone call he assumed the worst.

He mashed the garish purple phone's off button, and pulled the battery from its compartment. He walked slowly into his villa, dropped the pieces into the waste disposal, and ran the motor until any proof they ever existed was gone.

Enzo pulled a second phone from his pocket. A different model, a different carrier, a standard black color, purchased with cash from a different corner store.

He pressed the on button, and began making the calls required by the circumstances. He would make arrangements to meet the plane, then he would handle the disappearance of his brother.

Those who had been involved in Luigi's disappearance had made an error. A fatal one.

**FATAL ERROR is available now!**

# ABOUT THE AUTHOR

DIANE CAPRI is the *New York Times*, *USA Today*, and worldwide bestselling author. She's a recovering lawyer and snowbird who divides her time between Florida and Michigan. An active member of Mystery Writers of America, Authors Guild, International Thriller Writers, Alliance of Independent Authors, and Sisters in Crime, she loves to hear from readers and is hard at work on her next novel.

Please connect with Diane online:
http://www.DianeCapri.com
Twitter: http://twitter.com/@DianeCapri
Facebook: http://www.facebook.com/Diane.Capri1
http://www.facebook.com/DianeCapriBooks

Printed in the USA
CPSIA information can be obtained
at www.ICGtesting.com
CBHW020451240924
14769CB00002B/14